CHARLEY MILLS

COPYRIGHT:

PREFACE:

Seven Devils is a meditative psychological novel about endurance, false refuge, and the irrevocable transformations that follow when survival demands action. It contains depictions of emotional and physical abuse, trauma responses, and violence rooted in self-defense. These elements are integral to the psychological journey of the story and are presented with care rather than sensationalism. Reader discretion is advised.

ACKNOWLEDGEMENTS:

Thank you to the men and women of the Northern Ink Writers Group, in Grand Forks, North Dakota. Without their support and feedback, this project would probably still be unfinished. A very special thank you to K. A. Meng for taking the time, helping me revise the story for continuity and making sure I was making sense of a story that doesn't seem to make sense until the very end. Thank you to Emily for giving it a blind read and helping me expand on some points. To Darin, your patience and understanding throughout this writing process has been paramount to me completing it. Thank you for giving me the space I needed, when I needed it most. And thank you, to you, the reader, for being curious enough to join in on this journey.

LISTENING BONUS:

This soundtrack was developed alongside the novel, not after it.

Some scenes exist because of these songs, others were rewritten because the music revealed something the prose had not yet articulated.

The playlist is not a chapter guide. It is an emotional throughline—it is a psychological soundtrack meant to be experienced in sequence.

These songs do not just illustrate scenes. They inhabit spaces—where memory distorts, trust fractures, and survival requires cost.

There are moments of optimism, intimacy, and quiet—these are intentional. The human spirit needs them to continue forward; without them, nothing that follows would matter.

I recommend listening in order, without shuffle or interruption, and allowing the music to move ahead of you at times.

Not everything that feels safe remains so, and not every fight is chosen. Some are necessary.

Enjoy!

-Charley Mills

CHAPTER 1

"God, I fucking hate you!" I screamed into the phone as I turned away from the large moving box. "Seriously, why do you have to be like this?"

I was so tired of having this goddamn conversation with him. Again and again, repeatedly, I feel like I have been stuck in a loop for months now, my sanity nearly gone. I made sure to enunciate every syllable so there was no confusion with what I said next. "No! I am done with your bullshit. I am tired of you and I am exhausted by the nonsense. I truly, TRULY do not care anymore. I already told you, we are through, and I am leaving. There is nothing that you can say to stop that, so do yourself a favor and do not, call me, again."

Have you ever clenched your jaw so tight that your teeth hurt? I did. Hanging up the phone and shoving it into my back pocket, I screamed through gritted teeth and went back to packing up boxes. I didn't have time for him or the anger I felt because of him. I needed to calm down and get back to work. He just wasn't worth the time or energy.

My friend Robyn paused from helping me pack. "Diego?"

"Yes." I huffed.

"I am going to be sad to see you go," she said as she went back to wrapping up dinner plates in packing paper and placing them in a box, as she searched for a good excuse to get me to stay, "but honestly, it may be for the best."

I stopped and looked up momentarily. I wasn't ready for emotional goodbyes just yet, and honestly, I wasn't thinking about missing anyone. If I took the time to do that, I would most likely be a tragic mess right now. I lowered my head so my hair fell over my face and averted eye contact. I didn't want her to see the sadness there. "Thanks Robyn."

Robyn was a friend of mine from work. She was known for wearing scarves and a gaucho hat. Her lavender hair caught the light through the window as it fell in loose curls around her face. "No problem," she replied, as she went back to wrapping glasses in heavy paper and placing them in the box.

I was excited to get out of the city and move on to doing something different. Robyn was supportive of that, and I was going to miss her too, but there were always those that wanted to hold me back. This included my ex-boyfriend, Diego. He was not a decent person. He was the worst person I have ever dealt with, and I don't know why I let it go on as long as I had. Years had passed that he spent convincing me that I just wasn't good enough in life, in art, in love. He nearly convinced me that he was the best I was ever going to get. Luckily, I had a support group that eventually helped me see the psychological and emotional abuse he was putting me through.

It had taken me a couple of years, but I finally found my voice and my inner strength to fight back. After months of planning in secret, I found a home far from San Francisco and from him. I quit my job working for a fashion designer and was leaving to seek solitude and self-discovery. I would be leaving behind friends, lovers and the world I knew.

It will be difficult. I understand that there will be no safety net where I am headed. If I fail, I will be without a job or home and left wanting; but deep down I know, I need to be my own person again. I need to rediscover who I am, and work on being happy. Packing my things and moving to Bainbridge Island off the coast of the Puget Sound near Seattle, I could work on my own photography projects and start fresh, I hope. Nothing ever really goes the way we plan it though. Right?

After three days of packing, the moving company arrived. They took everything and I lived inside my empty room surrounded by take-out containers from my favorite spots in China Town and Little Italy, and trash bags full of paper plates and soda cans. Honestly, I lived like a squatter before the day came at the end of the week that my dog, Laika and I would get in the car and drive away.

It took us nearly a day to reach the destination, but getting there was entirely worth it. The island was quiet, except for the sounds of the ferry terminal, the gentle lapping of waves and the breeze through pine studded landscape. Children and adults biked around and it gave me a feel for the quiet, outdoorsy, simple kind of life here. It took mere moments to get my vehicle out of the ferry and drive to my new home. It was blue, surrounded by tall trees, and most of it was floor to ceiling windows. A second floor balcony with black railing stood out over what I was planning to make my home office.

I got out of the car and did one of those whole body stretches from my toes to my fingertips – you know, the kind that makes every muscle kind of shake for a moment. I even did some twists to get limber again. I inhaled, relishing the scent of the pine and sea. It was refreshing and clean; better than the air in San Francisco that was filled with sea salt, fecal matter, drugs, pretentiousness and misery. Laika ran around and looked for a place to relieve herself. I took my shoes off and walked through the grass, feeling it against my feet. For the first time, I actually had a lawn of my own.

My new home was a dream to behold. Floor to ceiling windows all around a geometrically shaped home painted blue to match the dusk, and blend into the night. I could imagine the way it would look when warm light radiated from inside, out. I wriggled my toes on the soft patch of earth I stood on.

Oh my god! This grass seriously feels like carpeting on my feet, and I love this short pier out back that leads out into the water of the Puget Sound. That will be nice to sit on in the summer, but I'm pretty sure the water is freezing, even then. I'll need to buy an Adirondack chair.

Finishing my walk, I was ready to explore inside. "Laika! Come!"

We raced inside, starting to pace from room to room. I surveyed, taking in each space and deciding on particular designs and layouts for each one while Laika sniffed every corner and crevice. I was wrapped up in my thoughts, and with a not so gentle reminder from my stomach, it was time to eat. Since I have to wait on my refrigerator delivery, there was nothing to eat here yet. I was going to have to take a ferry across to Seattle and grab something there and then get settled in the morning.

I remember passing a place called Dick's on the drive in. It had a line out the door – might be worth looking into.

Foggy morning light flooded the room in a cool grey at dawn, where Laika and I slept on the cold barren floor. Lucky for me, this huge snoring hound dog is good at keeping me warm. It was time to get up and start unpacking. I let Laika outside while I got cleaned up for the morning. The dog pawed at the door to be let inside when I came back downstairs. She was pretty good at that. She moved into the kitchen and rummaged through the fast food bags. I was mad at her for sniffing through the trash. It was a habit I could never break her of for the life of me. She was a rescue. I found her as a puppy scrounging through scraps to survive. I understand that old habits die hard, but it has been years. Maybe she was just a dog who loved trash. I mean, she was a bloodhound; they have exceptionally good noses. Still…

"I have a cheeseburger left if you want to split it?"

Her ears perked up and her head titled for a second. She smiled at me. *Bark bark, awoof.* She let out a headshaking sneeze.

"Of course you would," I smiled. Splitting the food in half and giving it to her, I patted her on the head. "I will get you some real food today, I promise."

I began to bite into my half when the doorbell rang. I covered my mouth as I chewed, muffling a rely, "Coming!"

I just got here last night, who could possibly be at my door? I never told anyone that I was moving here, and for a very good reason: I don't want to be found by anyone but myself. Opening the door, I was greeted by a smiling woman holding a casserole dish.

"Hi there! I know it's early, but I wanted to stop by and greet the new neighbor before I had to get my day going."

"Wow, people still do that?" I paused for a second as the woman was taken slightly aback. "I'm sorry, I didn't mean for that to come across so rude. Please come in."

Way to go Tara! You put your foot in your mouth in less than ten seconds. Congrats, you have a new record for being off putting.

The woman moved into the house, and I tried to recover the conversation. "It's just unusual for me to see someone bring welcoming gifts. I thought that kind of thing was only done in the movies anymore."

"Well, things are different all over the place, and not many of the neighbors here will. Everyone tends to keep to themselves for the most part, but I am not most people."

I escorted the woman to the kitchen where she set the casserole dish down on the counter. "I am Megan." Megan was a thin woman with medium stature. She was roughly the same age as me, in her mid-thirties. She had short, blonde, wavy hair and a toothy grin.

"Nice to meet you Megan, I'm Tara."

"So, what brings you to Bainbridge?"

How should I put this vaguely and politely?

"I just moved here wanting something new and quiet."

"Well, you've come to the right place. Heck! You can barely get cell service out here some days! The island stays quiet except for Mora's in the evening. Of course, there are also the festivals on the waterfront happening next summer. But you'll probably get a good view from out back."

"I look forward to it! It'll probably make for some cool shots."

"Sorry?"

"Oh, I'm a photographer."

"That's great! What kind?"

"Portrait, fashion and fine art mostly."

"Wonderful! I wouldn't mind seeing some of your work sometime."

"For sure! Once I get all set up here, I wouldn't mind having you over to see some."

"That would be fun." Megan smiled. "Well, I won't keep you any longer. I still need to catch the ferry over to Tillicum. Please, enjoy the casserole, and welcome to the neighborhood."

"Thank you, Megan. It was wonderful to meet you, and I'll see you again soon."

I immediately spun around as the door closed and went to find the portable speaker, setting up some music. Seriously, who doesn't work while listening to music anymore? It increases productivity. I was ready to go and then paused reflecting on Megan's words. I was unable to load my playlist from the phone as there was no cell service. Not being dismayed, I chose an album that had been saved on my device and began unpacking - starting with the kitchen. I got through all of the appliances which had a simple scheme of all white, and then I stowed away the cookware and utensils – less one fork to test the casserole.

I nodded unconsciously. "Green beans and porcini mushrooms. Good stuff." I set it aside, knowing this could heat up easily later, and continued unpacking, while beginning to think about what to buy to cook for dinner to go with that casserole.

I got through three of the rooms and had them set up before hunger kicked in and my back gave out. I may be young, still in my early thirties, but unpacking is brutal on the body. So, I decided it was time to take a break. I called out for Laika who was off exploring or sleeping again. We were going to check out Mora's real quick, and then hop on the ferry and check out Pike's Place Market to get some food. Also, we would stop at a local pet shop and pick up some supplies for Laika and a new toy or two for her to choose.

Returning that evening, Laika ran circles around me and barked repeatedly. That was out of character for her and had me concerned. "What's going on girl?" I asked, fumbling with my bags.

"Sorry to intrude!" a man called out stepping away from the front door. He fought off the cool weather with a leather jacket, a long scarf and dark denim jeans. Floppy hair fell across his face.

What the fuck? Who just creeps in the shadows of a stranger's house?

"That dog isn't going to bite me, is it?"

"That depends! Who are you?" I asked apprehensively while shuffling the bags in my arms, maintaining my distance.

"The name's Robert. People call me Robbie. I'm one of your neighbors." He stepped closer to the edge of the porch so I could see him better.

"Laika! Heel!" She returned to my side. "Good girl." I whispered. Her tongue hung out as she panted happily.

"It's nice to meet you Robbie, I'm Tara, but as you can see, I kind of have my hands full."

"Let me carry some of those for you," he said as he raced across the lawn. Laika growled at him and barked menacingly. He stopped dead in his tracks.

"Laika is not trusting of newcomers, especially men. We've had some unfortunate experiences," I mentioned to him. "You'll have to forgive us." I walked to the door and set my bags down and leaned against the outer wall. "What is it that I can do for you, Robbie?"

"I just wanted to come by and greet the new neighbor is all."

I shook my arms to loosen up the tense muscles from carrying the bags.

"You're not a creep, are you?"

"Not that I'm aware of," he said, taken aback. "But I guess that's also not for me to decide. I guess the real question here is, do you think I'm a creep?"

Clever guy, turning the tables.

I smiled despite my wariness. "I haven't decided. I could use some help with these bags though, if you'd like?"

"Sure." He smiled and grabbed the bags with ease and waited for me.

"Don't try anything funny, or I will empty my can of bear spray in your face. Got it?"

He laughed. "I promise you, I'm not that kind of guy."

"Uh huh." I looked at him cautiously as I opened the door and escorted him into the kitchen.

For the second time today, I brought a stranger into my home that I've been in for less than twenty-four hours.

Seriously, what the fuck is wrong with you, Tara? You are way too trusting. This is how you get murdered.

I immediately began putting things away and Robbie looked around. I monitored his movements with the precision of a Peregrine falcon. Spotting the casserole dish he replied, "I see Megan was here."

"Yes, she stopped by this morning. Very friendly woman."

"That she is," Robbie stated as he set the bags down on the island countertop.

I am not sure how I should interpret that response.

Shaking it off, I moved on while putting away groceries. "Tell me Robbie, and no offense in advance, but why did you come here?"

"Like I said, to say hi, and greet the new neighbor." He started to unpack the bags and set things out on the counter in groups – fresh food, cans, dry goods, etc.

"I was told that most of the neighbors keep to themselves."

"We do. But that doesn't mean I still can't be polite." He smiled with a tinge of sass.

I rolled my eyes as I turned to put things in the fridge. "And what do you do for a living, Robbie?"

"I work as an architectural repair specialist."

Pausing for a second, I thought about it. "You're a construction worker?"

"If that's what you want to call it in layman's terms, sure. I work with rebuilding the structural integrity and updating the design of buildings during remodels and work on restoring older buildings to their former glory."

"Oh. That's cool."

"What about you?"

"Photographer."

"You were able to afford this place on a photographers' salary?"

"That's fucking rude!" I snapped.

There was a moment of silence between us as the air was charged with intensity. Robbie noticed and tried to be disarming.

"Sorry, I didn't mean it to be. It's just that this place has a pretty big price tag attached to it. If you don't mind me asking, how did you afford it?"

Seriously? The same way anyone else does, asshole!

"By saving. I just moved from San Francisco where rent is exceptionally expensive. I shared a slightly spacious place with four other people which made living more affordable and comfortable. I was able to put away for a rainy day. Also, the cost of living here is cheaper than it is in San Francisco."

While he wasn't paying attention, I grabbed my bear spray and bunched it in my hand, ready to use as necessary. There was a feeling in the pit of my stomach, and I wanted to be prepared.

"That's," he paused, "something. I don't think I could live in a place with four other people."

"I'm going to take a guess that you don't have any family here?" I started asking questions in a rapid fire pace.

"No, I do. I just don't have a large one. It's only me and my wife."

"No kids?"

"Nope."

He leaned against the island, crossed his arms and smiled.

"Planning on any?"

"No," he laughed. "Neither of us want any. The world seems too populated with madness and strife, so we chose not to bring another being into it. Besides, my wife is constantly travelling which could be tough on raising a child. What about you, Tara? Any significant other or family in your life?"

I put my thumb on the trigger of the bear spray behind my back. "It's just me and Laika for right now."

"I can understand the momentary solitude. You know, I used to come here when I needed a break, and just sit on the pier, or sit in that front room and stare out the windows." He moved about reminiscing then looked at me with a deadpan expression. His mouth twitched into a smile and returned to a normal straight line position.

Oh, my, fucking god! This guy is going to hurt me, isn't he? He wants his house back!

My hands shook. I was scared, and what's worse is, I did this to myself.

Should I just spray him in the face now? I did warn him in advance.

Taking a ragged breath, I tried to keep the situation from escalating. Maybe he wasn't a bad guy and I was overreacting from past trauma.

"When did you do all that?" I asked as calmly as possible, putting the island directly between the two of us and creating a barrier space without drawing attention to what I was doing.

"A few years back when the place was being remodeled for the old owner to sell. Floor to ceiling windows are not an easy thing to install. It sure did change how this place looks though. I dig it."

"Same here. I guess I should say thank you." I kept my hand ready with the spray behind my back and moved to lean back against the kitchen sink.

"No problem," he smiled. "Anyway, I won't intrude any longer. I just wanted to make my presence known. Hopefully I will see you around?"

"Sure."

"We have a group of locals that meet at a bar on Wednesday nights for trivia if you're ever interested. Just stop by and let me know. I'm in the green house down the street."

Robbie saw himself out. As the front door closed, I quietly locked it, and then calmly made my way behind another closed door where I fell to my knees and cried. As the terror and the tremors subsided, I cleaned up my appearance to make myself and Laika dinner. Afterwards, I unpacked a couple more boxes of all white bedroom décor, so I had some clean sheets to sleep on before calling it a night.

The next day, I finished the remainder of unpacking; keeping things simple and clean in every room with the white theme throughout. Also, it gives the illusion of a space being bigger than it is. Furniture was set up in way that allowed for easily walkable paths from one room to the next without having to sidestep anything. The couch and high back chairs all faced away from the windows towards the interior of the house. I always thought that it gave a sense of minimalism, serenity, purity and cleanliness.

The office was slightly different though. In there, I had a mixture of black, white and gray, because some office furniture just doesn't come in white. Chairs were black and gray. The easels were all black and steel. The design tablet I used was black and it set next to an all white computer that I built myself on a white desk. As I unpacked my art pieces and set them around the room, they give the space more life with pops of colors. I hooked up the gallery lights to each easel and turned them on and the overhead room light off. This gave the space a cozier feel. After finishing up, I pulled a sweater on and relaxed on the back porch with Laika long into the evening, listening to the waves and the horn of the ferry boat as it went by.

I sat in my new Adirondack chair with a glass of wine and started to review places available to rent studio space. I compiled a list to check out the next day. If all went well, I may have the foundation for my new life set up in about a week and some change.

In the morning, I crossed Elliott Bay again. The streets of the Seattle area were busy, but not crowded like back in San Francisco. It was nice to not have to walk in the street to avoid overcrowded sidewalks, or bump shoulders with a complete stranger and not say anything. There weren't a ton of one-way streets, side streets and alleyways either, making navigating the downtown area much easier. However, much like back in the bay area, parking was still a commodity.

I ended up having to park near the aquarium, not too far from the ferry terminal. From there, most of the places I was looking at, were within walking distance if you consider a few square miles walking distance. Let's face it, walking long distances isn't an issue for me when I've grown accustomed to having to park halfway across a city and use my own two feet and public transit for years. A few of the other sites I wanted to see were on the fringes of the city, and I decided to check those out last.

I pulled out the list of places to see, marking them off as I viewed them with two different realtors – Shawn and Peter. I added notes to my journal as we went. In total, I saw thirteen different properties. Ten properties I discarded easily due to the area and appearances. Not to say that the interiors were all that bad, but graffiti, crime, homelessness and drug use proliferation in the area surrounding the properties were an absolute deal breaker for me. Three listings, I expected to go back to and look at once more before deciding. I took plenty of pictures of the spaces–both interior and exterior to help me make the best decisions of what I needed and what I liked best.

It took a big part of my afternoon to get through the list before making my way back to the car, shivering in the looming wind. The cold front was moving faster than I expected and the air chilled. My breath began to appear before me in puffs of mist as I exhaled. Fog rolled over the waterfront and along the levies quickly, blanketing the city in a haze that slowed everything down. This quick change was absolutely nuts!

The drive back to the ferry from the aquarium wasn't far, but I was going to take my time. Even in San Francisco, I avoided driving in the fog. Hopefully tomorrow would be clear, and I can have another productive day of studio space reviews and sight-seeing in the city. For now, I was thinking it was going to be a tomato soup and grilled cheese kind of night.

Laika joined me on the couch as the blue light of the television washed over us in the dark. A light amber glow emanated from a salt lamp in the corner providing us with comfort and a little bit of warmth. I was busy perusing movies and shows to watch, all the while the dog did her best to take a bite of my sandwich. She was scolded and resigned herself to laying down beside me with her pitiful puppy dog eyes pleading for food, despite already having been fed. I scratched behind her ears and patted her head until she snored on my lap. Eventually I found something to watch, and soon after that, I joined Laika in slumbering on the couch.

CHAPTER 2

Gray dawn filled the bedroom again. Laika licked my face trying to wake me up to go outside. Grumbling, I hugged her close until she squirmed to get away. "Alright, alright. I will get up."

She bounded towards the door and barked happily, tail wagging so much her body began to sway back and forth. The door opened, and she darted into the mist. My eyes were bleary, unable to really make out the Puget Sound. I tried to clear them and that didn't work, but I was able to hear the waves and horn of the ferries. I couldn't stay outside for long though. The mist was cold, surprising me even though I came from the bay area where the mist was cold too, but not like this. Back in California, when the fog rolled in, you could just feel the moisture in the air. Here, it felt like ice, and it hurt my face. I moved back indoors to drape myself in a blanket. I was unsure of whether I would become accustomed to the cold of the north even though it wasn't winter yet.

I started my morning by getting coffee going, sniffing the air as the aroma of the beans wafted around, and bread was toasting. I waited to wake up by propping myself up against the counter when I heard a loud thump. Laika was sitting at the back door. She barked and pawed at the glass again wanting to come back in. I couldn't help but roll my eyes as I retrieved her. I loved this mutt. Shortly after, breakfast was ready and it was time to go again for the day. I grabbed my phone and called Shawn, while sipping my coffee against the counter.

"Hello, Shawn? It's Tara. I came by the other day to look at studio spaces for lease." I leaned against the sink and took another sip and set my mug down. "I was wondering if you had time today to allow me to come in for a second look?"

I pushed off the edge and wandered around the island, drumming my fingers as I went. "Okay, what time works best for you? Sounds good. Thanks again Shawn, I'll see you this afternoon."

I disconnected the call and did a little happy dance. Laika watched curiously. One of the few spaces was still on the market. There was still one more person to contact that showed me a couple of places. His card was buried in my purse among all my other goodies. The phone rang several times before a voice picked up but then cut out.

"Hello, Peter? Are you there?"

"Yes," his voice crackled.

"Oh good! I am having trouble with service out here. I was hoping that I could set up a time with you to go look at two of the spaces I viewed the other day?"

"Tara? Can you hear me?"

"Peter?" I checked the phone for signal strength. "Peter. If you can hear me, I will call you back in about an hour."

The phone call went silent. I am not sure I can live somewhere with little phone service. I stuffed the phone in my pocket and grabbed a coat, scratched Laika behind the ears and kissed her on the head before leaving the house and heading back across the way into the city.

Calling Peter again after disembarking the ferry, I set up a time to see the two properties. There was just enough time for me to check out all three studios, and a couple of spots for potential photo shoots before having to head back home. The first stop was to see him. He stood just under six feet tall. His eyes were green and his hair copper. He dressed fashionably well in a tweed suit, no tie.

The first property was in the Industrial District. I liked it because it was close to the highway. The property had east and west facing windows which would allow a lot of natural light in during the golden and blue hours for portrait work. However, at the same time, it would become an issue if I wanted more control over the lighting set-ups, I may need a place that is more enclosed. I let Peter know that this location was no longer a viable option for me.

The second property was northeast of the city in Sand Point just north of Pontiac. This one was once a garage that had been revamped. There were shutters on the doors so I could let light in if I wanted, the doors were facing north and south. The location was a bit out of the way, but it was also close to an art school that worked with the University of Washington, and I might be able to advertise for interns at some point. However, I wasn't too sure whether or not I wanted this studio location entirely because the drive may be a factor.

"I'm not so sure," I eluded. "I like the place, but I still have one more to go look at later today. Can I give you a call this evening, and let you know?"

"Absolutely," Peter replied. "Take your time. And thank you again for calling me to let me know that you were interested."

"Thanks," I smiled as I headed back to my car. The last spot I needed to check out was in the middle of the city. It is within walking distance of most things I need–food, entertainment, parks and such. I got there early like I tend to do with most appointments and waited for Shawn.

While passing the time, I looked around the neighborhood and dreamt of the possibilities. It wasn't far from an art gallery and I could potentially commission work with them. If I wanted to go out at night after work, it was only a couple blocks from anything major. Granted, I still need to drive back and forth from the ferry terminals. The location was in an annexed portion of an old church which gave the place character. The windows were large, facing north and south but could be shuttered and the hardwood floors with white walls were inspiring. Different art projects spiraled through my mind as I took in the area.

"Tara!" a voice called from across the street.

Whipping my head around I waved, "Shawn! Great to see you!"

"It is great to see you again too," he responded as he neared and shook my hand. The best way, I could describe this man, was a silver fox. He was tall and fit, muscular, but not broad. His hair was salt and pepper gray with eyes of steel blue. He moved with confidence and smiled with sincerity. "Thanks for reaching out to me again about this space. I'm excited that it made your list of revisits. Are there any questions that you have about the place or the area that need to be addressed?"

"Actually, yes. I do have a few," I said as I pulled out my notebook and flipped the pages to the last one I wrote on.

"Alright. Lay it on me."

"What is the crime rate like in this area of town? I know what it is for Seattle in general, but with a lot of expensive camera and lighting equipment, I want to budget for necessary security measures if needed."

"Good question!" He pulled out his phone and brought up a document as he continued talking. "The crime report was released by the police department earlier this year, showing that this area is one of the ten safest neighborhoods in Seattle. Granted, if you go a couple of blocks in any direction, that is subject to change."

With a brief pause, he started reading directly from the document and showed me so I could read along. "The rates for violent crimes are less than one for every thousand people. The rates of robbery are just over two in every thousand people."

He put his phone away and continued to talk, looking me in the eye intently. "This isn't to say that you should let your guard down though. If you are thinking about security for yourself or your new studio, a standard system that can access 911 immediately should do you justice. Also, make sure that your insurance coverage is up to date for health and personal property."

"Good to know."

"Of course. Anything else?"

"How much do you know about power billing?"

"I wouldn't say I know everything, but I can try to answer or find an answer for you if I don't know it. What's the question?"

"I rolled my eyes as the words came off my lips. "Well, coming from California, our power companies had this wonderful idea to raise rates frequently. They charge more for air conditioning in the summer, and more for heating in the winter."

My voice became more agitated and I crossed my arms as I continued. "On top of that, there were the peak hour premium rates where they would basically charge you double, sometimes triple the normal price just because of the time of day that you would use either. Is that an issue here as well?"

"Not to the extent of price gouging like that. Walk with me," he said. The two of us wandered down the street conversing as he led the way to a coffee shop. "The utility companies here do have peak usage hours listed where they charge more, but they aren't double or triple. It's a percentage more but normally about ten percent on top of the price for the season. One of the great things about this property and area is that it doesn't get too hot. However, a whole-house fan system has been installed to help keep cooling costs low. It also helps circulate warm air in the winter."

"Awesome! Are there any rules governing subletting, or potentially running a co-op? I am sure that it will just be me in the studio, but the thought has crossed my mind about renting out studio space by the hour to increase revenue."

He ordered two mochas for us to take on the go and paid for them, thanking the barista before turning his attention back to me.

"There are some guidelines about subletting for this space since it is leased to you directly. Running a co-op or renting space by the hour shouldn't be an issue but we can go over all of that during paperwork signing and address it in more detail if need be. However, you may want to talk to your insurance company about any additional coverages you may need to do something like that."

"I will definitely do that then. Last question for you."

"Alright," he replied.

"Is the price set in stone or can we work a deal to bring it down a bit?"

We picked up our drinks from the end of the counter. I left a tip in a jar, and we made our way back out to the street.

"How much are we talking?"

"You have it listed at four thousand a month. Since my business is not entirely established yet, I was hoping to get it down to three thousand or thirty-five hundred at least."

His pace slowed as he pondered it. "I think that would be doable. I can't commit to anything yet. Once I get back to the office, I can crunch some numbers and give you a call if that's alright?"

"That would be great, thank you! I would love to have this place."

"Not a problem. Let me get some numbers for you, and hopefully we can have you sign some paperwork in the next day or so."

We returned to exactly where we started and I faced him. "Thank you so much Shawn! For the insight, help and the coffee."

I beamed with excitement as I shook his hand. My cheeks ached from smiling so widely, and then we went about our way. That evening a call from Shawn came through confirming that he could get the space down to three thousand a month for the first year if I needed it.

Oh my god, yes please!

That night wine flowed and dancing around the living room was required for celebration. Laika joined by jumping up and swaying with me from side to side as I held her front paws. We exhausted ourselves and slept soundly until the next morning when she licked my face to wake me up again.

Pushing her off, I got up and dressed. One of the first things I needed to do today was get Laika a doggy door. Granted, I don't have the necessary tools or skills to install one, so I definitely need to ask for help. Laika was outside sniffing around again as I brewed coffee, thinking of who I could contact to help. In the distance, the sound of a motorcycle revving tickled my eardrums and slowly reached its crescendo as Robbie rode down the road. I just heard and watched my answer drive by.

The day breezed by faster than I expected as I kept busy. Between pet shops, hardware stores, the realtor office, coffee shops and marketplace, I soon realized that it was getting dark. Checking my phone for my daily to-do list, I realized that I never called Peter back.

"Shit, shit, shit!" Cursing myself, I dialed his number. "Please pick up."

"Hello?"

"Peter?"

"Yes."

"Hi Peter, it's Tara."

"Good to hear from you again. How are you?"

"I am doing alright Peter, thanks for asking. I meant to call you back yesterday, but it slipped my mind. I apologize for that."

"No worries. Did you make a decision?"

"Yes. Unfortunately, I will not be going for either of the properties I saw."

"That is unfortunate, but I respect your decision. Thank you for calling to let me know."

"Of course. Thank you again Peter. Take care."

"You too."

My shoulders slumped, and eyes closed partially as I heaved a heavy sigh. It sucks to have to give people bad news, but it is just a part of business, and life. I headed home.

Dinner baked in the oven, and I poured myself some wine.

Note to self: buy more wine.

I was looking at some of my artwork that rested on easels. I savored the drink in my glass as I reflected on the images and pondered its deeper meaning, trying to find an elusive truth. One day it may reveal itself to me, but I don't think I am at a point yet where I can see it. Even worse still, I wasn't sure I was looking at the works, or if they were looking at me. One thing was for certain, I was intrinsically a part of the project and saw personal flaws in it. Taking another concerted look at the pieces, I turned my back on them.

The timer on the counter garnered my attention for a moment; I had time. Grabbing a coat and scarf, I headed down the street to make two stops. First, I walked down the road at a brisk pace to arrive at the green house down the street with the American flag on a pole out front with a well-manicured lawn. The doorbell chimed under the pressure of my fingertip and I stepped back and waited.

The door opened, washing me in warm white light and the scent of vanilla. "Wow! That smells good," I reacted.

"Yes? Can I help you?"

I found myself face to face with a woman in her mid-thirties. She had long black hair braided to one side and tucked under her apron. Her bronze skin glistened except in spots where covered with flour.

"Hello. I'm sorry to interrupt you. My name is Tara, I just moved into the house down the road about a week ago. I wanted to introduce myself."

"That's very thoughtful of you. I'm Kiera." She reached out a hand coated in flour and I shook it.

"Nice to meet you Kiera," I smiled.

"You as well. Look, not to be rude, but I am in the middle of baking right now. Is there something I can help you with?"

"Oh. No worries. Um, is Robbie around by chance?"

"Just a minute, I'll go grab him. Sorry again for being short, hopefully we can chat more another time."

"Of course! Thank you."

I kept checking my watch, keeping track of the minutes left when Robbie waltzed towards the door in jeans and a white tee.

"Good to see you again Tara. What's up?"

"Hey, I don't know any handy men and since your background is in design construction, I was hoping you might be able to help me with a project?"

"What's the project?"

"I need to install a doggy door for Laika. I don't have any tools *or* much experience with power tools." His smile was radiant. I never noticed it before. Just the second I admitted that I wasn't good with tools, I saw it. There was a bit of a laugh behind the smile, and it was infectious. I couldn't stop myself and reciprocated earnestly. "Is that a yes?"

"Sure," he chuckled. "When do you want my help?"

"If you have free time later tonight, or tomorrow, that would be great."

"I can come by in the morning about eight if that works?"

"Definitely! Thank you again."

"Robbie!" Kiera called. "Can you help me please? I have too many cookies to cut out by myself!"

"Sure thing honey!" he called back over his shoulder. "I should get going. See you tomorrow?"

"Yeah. Oh! One last thing though. Where does Megan live?"

"Just down the road, the house on the right with a red door!" He shouted after me as I walked away.

"Thanks Robbie. See you later."

"Later!" he called shutting the door.

I trotted down the road, my eyes piercing the night for the splash of color in the sea of darkness. There weren't many streetlights out here, which was nice because it allowed me to see the stars – something I could never have done in San Francisco unless I took a trip up to Goat Rock, or down towards Pacifica. Like a beacon before me was a red the shade of a ripe, delicious apple. Stepping up to it, I rang the bell and waited for Megan.

When the door opened, Megan's eyes went wide in surprise.

"Hi Tara! I wasn't expected to see you."

"Is this a bad time?"

"No, not at all. What can I help you with?"

"Well, I wanted to repay the favor of you bringing me a dish that first day. I was wondering if you'd like to join me for dinner and then take a look at some of my artwork before I have it moved to the new studio space tomorrow."

"Like, right now?"

"Yes. Unless you're busy. I would totally understand since this was a very last-minute decision."

"No, I wouldn't mind at all. Give me a minute to change?"

"Sure." I smiled.

"Okay, I'll be right back."

We returned to my place just in time. The timer on the counter went off, and I grabbed dinner out of the oven. Opening the door, the blast of heat hit my face making me flinch. The gentle sizzling and bubbling of sauces wafted across the room as the scent of melted mozzarella and parmesan invaded our noses. Laika came to investigate.

I set it on the stove to rest for a bit and poured a couple glasses of wine for Megan and myself. "Thank you again for coming over."

"No, thank you for inviting me. To be honest, I felt like I may have offended you in some way. If I did, I apologize."

"No, not at all. You coming over that first day was surprising, but it showed your genuine nature, and I appreciate that. I would have invited you sooner, but I needed to get my life set up first."

"Understandable," she said with a slow nod.

"Shall we eat?"

Laika barked happily in reply.

"Not you, tubby!" I called back.

Megan and I shared a laugh. Laika bowed her head and laid down. She huffed, looking back and forth wondering if either of us would cave and share a bite of our dinner. We laughed again.

"What are we having?"

"Homemade lasagna and a spinach salad." I replied.

"Sounds delicious."

We continued to converse for some time, discussing life on the island and in the area. I filled Megan in on what I'd been doing the last couple of days here while I was getting set up. We talked about our pasts on a bit of a deeper level and grew an understanding of one another. Finally, we chatted about aspirations in our lives. Megan was working on a doctoral degree in Marine Biology. I was wanting to one day get back into school and work on my MFA in photography. I hoped that after establishing myself as an artist, I could get a teaching credential to help flourish the next generation of artists at the collegiate level.

"That's an admirable goal."

"Thank you. I am hoping that this new project of mine is good enough to make a mark. Speaking of which, if you are ready, I could show you what I've been working on."

Megan wiped her mouth and nodded with excitement. "I'd love to."

I escorted her across the living room and down the hallway to a room on the back side of the house. Before opening the door, I gave Megan a warning.

"So, what I'm going to show you, may not be your cup of tea. I have been told by some, that it is frightening and unsettling in its own right. I only ask that you have an open mind, and be honest with your feedback."

Skeptically, she agreed, and I let her in the room. Scattered about were thirteen easels, each highlighted by a spotlight pointed at them. On these easels were large, twenty-four by thirty-six inch images on dense foam core. At first, Megan only noticed that each one was a different block of color from the other. Then as she got closer, she saw things. The images were staring back at her. The eyes were prominent. She started to notice the rest of the features – arms, lips, hair, faces that weren't fully formed or colored like a human body. Parts of the bodies were missing and what was there was in shades of black and white with pops of color in hues of reds and oranges. It captivated and held her gaze.

"What do you think?" I asked as I stood beside her, taking a drink.

She struggled to find the words. Finally, she admitted in the best way she could, "It's haunting. What exactly am I looking at?"

"Before I answer that, will you do me the favor of telling me what you think you're looking at? If I tell you first, it could change your perception, and I want yours to remain as pure as possible for now."

"Sure, I'll take a stab at it." She walked around the room sipping her wine, taking in the images once more and contemplating.

"Um, if I was honest with myself, I get this feeling like I'm seeing something that isn't real. I mean, I know it's not, but it feels like it's of another realm, like what I would see in a nightmare. Not to say that it's terrifying in a bad way, but it looks like a human either emerging from or dissolving into this pool of color."

"Okay," I said drawing out the sound as I leaned against my work desk. "So how does it make you feel?"

"Unsettled," she affirmed as she turned towards me. "What about you?"

"It makes me feel like I don't know who I am." I stared directly at one of the images, with a terracotta colored background.

Megan looked at me a little perplexed, and also saddened. It's not the first time I've seen that look, and I'm sure it won't be the last, but that's alright. I just stared ahead at the prints and took a sip of wine before continuing.

I moved slowly from one easel to another contemplating the artwork again. "I started this series a couple of years ago and have continued it because I haven't uncovered its whole truth yet. I am hoping that one day it will reveal itself."

Stopping in front of the orange image, I stared with scrutiny at a female figure with red and yellow marks in various spots, even some darker brown ones on her face and neck. "It's a weird thing about art that I've found. We create and we create, simply based off of some muse, but the intention of it and purpose is sometimes elusive. I love this series to death! I just wish I understood the antithesis of it."

When I was done staring, I turned back towards Megan and ushered her to a chair beside me at my desk. "I used to work as a fashion photographer and image retoucher for a major clothing brand in San Francisco." Turning my computer one, I opened one of my art files to walk her through it. "One day, I was editing a picture, with this program that I use. It allows you to create a bunch of invisible layers which are like pieces of paper stacked together to edit a photograph without destroying the original. I accidentally hid the original image and that's how I saw something similar to these images."

I pressed a button and showed her what I meant. Megan made an audible sound and then took another drink of wine. "That's impressive and very interesting. I didn't know so much went into this," she replied.

I nodded. "Every edit I ever made to someone's face was showcased when I did this, but not the original picture. I stared at it for a long time, and my mind went blank. The fashion and advertising industry lies to us every single day. Not a single one of the photos you see aren't edited in some way, and here I was, face to face with the lie no one else notices. All of the changes I made were clearly in focus and it created this life of its own-a ghost of the original image. But that's when I questioned if it was the ghost of the image, or an entity all its own. Or was it just my own reflection?"

She turned her head away from the screen and looked at the easels once more. Standing, she paced by each one with a more discerning gaze. "Which do you think it is?" Megan asked as she stared at the haunting image of a man leaning forward against a green background. His hands were detailed in black, his eyes were a piercing white curve and his cheeks were pink. A flesh tone band marked his forehead.

"I'm still not entirely sure. It's weird that every image is of a different person, and you never see the actual person, but you do see their resemblance. Additionally," I sighed. "I see myself, because I understand that every mark, every correction is a glimpse into my mind of what I felt needed to be changed. Which allows me to view it not only as a ghost of the individual, but a ghost of the self and of self-consciousness."

"A very profound statement. I love it." She stared at an image on another green background. This one darker in shade, but with a prominent face and white orbs for eyes.

"Really?" I was grateful for the understanding and also surprised that she was able to comprehend my thought process.

"Yeah! Now that you've said that, I get it." Her head titled from side to side while taking it in. "It's a refreshing reflection of what industry beauty standards are and how that has infiltrated and affected the mind of the creator."

I smiled and nodded. Finally, someone gets it!

Megan queried whether or not I was going to try and have a gallery showing of this work. I wanted to, and the studio I leased was near an art gallery and college. I was hoping that I could, as soon as I made a handful of other images.

"I do have another question though, because it doesn't make sense to me." Megan continued.

"Alright."

"What's up with the colored backgrounds?"

"Originally, the backgrounds were all gray which made them all look really like photographic negatives and ghosts at the same time. I have one over here that you can see." I showed her one of the originals in the corner for reference. It was of a young woman, taken from a low angle with her arms crossed, but the corrections gave it a depiction of religious iconography.

"I wanted to experiment with color and the feelings that each one evokes. I eventually settled on these, and you can see that each one gives off a perception that is reflective of the positioning of the models and the overall mood of what the image should be."

"I don't quite get what you mean..." Her head shook with confusion.

"Each colored background is a mood reflected in the model. I was hoping that each one would make you feel slightly different when you look at them, so you understood more of the model than myself."

"Got it. Well, I have to say, that this wasn't what I was expecting at all, but I am impressed."

"Thank you." I replied sincerely.

"No Tara, thank you for sharing this with me. It shows a lot about you, and I hope we can be good friends."

"Me too Megan." I gave her a hug and we exited the room for more wine and food.

As the night grew longer, Megan took her leave after exchanging phone numbers and I cleaned up and prepared for bed. Before I did though, I went back to my home workspace. I turned on my studio lights and camera before taking a seat in the center of the room. I positioned my body and then slouched forward ever so slightly. My gaze was straight toward the camera, staring directly at the aperture of the lens, my expression, forlorn and betraying the internal exhaustion I felt. Clicking the remote trigger in hand, I snapped a photograph of myself, and then three more. Each one I took, I changed my position slightly, but my face always remained the same. Maybe by using myself as a subject in this project from a different phase in my life, I could come to a new revelation regarding the work. Who knows?

Satisfied with the shots, I spent the next hour editing and making an initial print before shutting everything down and going upstairs. Laika snuggled up by my side.

The whirring of a power drill stirred me awake. Laika bolted from the room baying until she came to Robbie, continuing to bark at him through the glass door. I waved at him even though I looked like a wreck and pulled her back by the collar to get her fed. After getting coffee brewed, I let her out and spoke to Robbie as I handed him a mug.

"Thank you for coming over and doing this. Sorry for all the barking."

"Not a problem." He grabbed the cup. "I hope it works. I know it takes some time for dogs to adjust to these doggie doors."

"I'll work with her on it. It shouldn't be too hard."

"Well, you are all set. Also, I put a latch on it, so you can lock the door at night or when you're gone if need be."

"Thank you so much!"

"Yup." Robbie nodded. "Anything else you need?"

With a small shake of the head, Robbie was done. He took another long drink and passed my mug back. "Right. Well, if you need anything, you know how to get a hold of me."

After taking a few steps, he turned and called back. "Hey! Tonight, we are meeting for trivia, hope to see you there!"

"Where?"

"The Blarney Stone!" he waved before turning and leaving all together.

I whistled for Laika who busied herself sniffing the sand at the end of the walkway to the shore. She trotted my way and we went inside together. I grabbed a few treats and set my focus on training her to use the door to get in and out.

At first, she was hesitant as she didn't like the flap hitting her in the face, but she soon adjusted to knowing it can be pushed out of the way. Soon she realized she was free to come and go through this door. After a little bit of training, I was confident that Laika understood how to use the new feature.

I prepared to go. I had to pack camera equipment, artwork, and props before going to see Shawn so I could sign paperwork, get the keys and start the move-in process for the new studio.

Sometimes being an adult sucks ass. Today was one of those days. The morning was mundane and filled with an exorbitant amount of paperwork. I was going to have carpel tunnel syndrome from all the signatures I gave. The afternoon was spent setting up utilities and by late afternoon, I had arrived at the studio and began unpacking.

I was already exhausted by then, not physically, but mentally exhausted which feels worse most days. I set everything inside a closet for now, covered it with a blanket, and locked the doors before exiting the studio and locking those doors as well.

Tomorrow was going to be the first real day of working in the studio, but for now, I needed to find this bar for some trivia night with friends. It was near the ferry terminal, which was nice, so getting back home wouldn't be too hard.

Inside, I slipped onto a stool at the counter and ordered an icy cold brew to pass the time waiting for anyone I knew to show up. I drummed my nails on the bar repeatedly, traced the condensation droplets on the outside of my second glass, and sighed by the time my third drink arrived. It had been nearly half an hour and I was ready to just give up, eat and leave. I decided to give them some more time.

"Excuse me?" I called to the bartender, a tattooed woman in her forties who was filling a beer from the tap. "Can I get a menu?"

She passed me a menu from behind the counter and said to let her know when I was ready to order. Perusing the options, a familiar voice called from behind. "Decide on anything good?"

Turning around, I saw Robbie and his wife, Kiera. "Hey there! Glad to see some familiar faces. Kiera, it's good to see you again."

"Same here."

"How are you guys doing?" I asked.

"Not too bad. What about you?" she asked. There was something in her tone when she said that–a sort of indifference that I thought I sensed but let slide.

"Well, I got my new photography studio lease signed today, and moved a lot of things over, so I'm feeling pretty good about that."

"That sounds like a lot of work. Good for you!. I didn't know you were a photographer."

"Well, you and I haven't really had the chance to sit and get to know one another yet."

"That's true," she sighed.

"Hopefully, tonight will change that a bit?"

"Sure," Kiera smiled.

Robbie ordered drinks for him and his wife. I ordered some appetizers to share, and the three of us went to another room and sat at a round table. "The rest of them should be here in a bit," Robbie assured.

My food arrived and I dug into a plate full of nachos telling Robbie and Kiera to help themselves. Both graciously declined.

"So, I have never played trivia before," I admitted. "Anything I should know?"

"Not really," Robbie said. "They go over the rules before the game begins."

"You've never played trivia before?" Kiera asked incredulously.

"Nope." I smiled innocently.

"Wow! What did you do with your friends for fun before moving here?"

"I guess the usual stuff? We would hang out at bars and nightclubs, catch the occasional show down in the Castro or concert at the Civic Centre. But mostly, we all just worked."

"Huh. Is San Francisco really that high paced?"

"I can't really say. I know for me and my friends, the answer was yes. We worked in the fashion industry, so it's always go, go, go. Silicon Valley techies had a worse schedule than us, but for the average resident, I'm not sure."

"You weren't an average resident?" she asked slightly amused.

"No, I was an average resident, with an above average career."

"So why did you leave it behind?"

I paused and reflected. Diego's face flashed in my mind. The dark Hispanic features, full head of hair and tattoos. Eyes that pierced the soul. "I needed my sanity."

"And how's that going for you?"

"Just fine, thanks." I was starting to get irritated. Kiera was getting to know me, but despite my openness on the matter, it felt intrusive and aggressive. Taking the opportunity to keep things from getting heated, I asked Kiera a question.

"Are you from Seattle, Kiera?"

"No."

"Where are you from?"

"Bend, Oregon."

"What made you decide to move?"

"College."

Okay, no more letting it slide. This is too much.

"Kiera, are you okay? When you first came in, everything was fine, but now you seem a bit short, and I'm not sure if it's something I did."

Kiera stared daggers at me. She took a deep breath and got up announcing that she was going to get another drink.

"Sweetie, you already have one here," Robbie stated.

"Not what I meant." She snapped back and walked to the bar to pound a few shots.

"What is going on?" I asked in wonderment.

Robbie shook his head. "Sometimes she's like this. Kiera has a tendency to try to keep people at arms-reach, so she gives short answers. She's been snippy off and on all day. I think it has something to do with her grant being denied."

"Grant for what?"

"You'd have to ask her, but tonight wouldn't be a good time to ask."

"Oh. Was it a work or study grant?"

"Both. Kiera is an anthropologist."

"Neat! That would definitely explain questions while keeping a distance. It's like she was studying me."

"Oh, she totally was." Robbie laughed and took a swing of beer before helping himself to the nachos.

I laughed too. "Good to know."

"Hey guys!" Megan called, teeth gleaming. "Sorry I'm late."

"It's alright," Robbie said. "The game hasn't started yet."

"I brought one of my friends with me, if you don't mind. Robbie, Tara, meet Collin. Collin, this is Robbie and Tara."

Collin was a strapping man. He had broad shoulders and dirty blond hair. He had a slightly rounded face giving him a boyish quality to him, but his eyes and strong chin gave him a manly edge. He smiled and I immediately reciprocated it. I was infatuated with his appearance.

The group exchanged pleasantries and had a seat.

"Where's Kiera?" Megan asked.

"Doing shots at the bar," Robbie muttered.

"Bad day?" Megan asked.

"No, it wasn't a bad day." Kiera interrupted. "I'm sorry I was short with you, Tara. It's good to see you, Megan."

Megan stood and hugged her friend. "Good to see you too. Kiera. Meet my friend Collin."

Collin stood to greet Kiera and then sat again.

"So why are you doing shots by yourself?" Megan asked.

"My grant request was denied."

"That sounds like a bad day," Megan tried to justify.

"No, not a bad day. Just a bad event. The rest of my day was just fine."

"Oh my god! You do that to?" I asked excitedly.

"What?" Megan asked, utterly confused by my glee. Kiera's eyes darted to mine, wide with surprise.

"Compartmentalized judgement! It's a mental practice that helps you better control your emotions and outlooks in life! If I had a bad day, multiple things would have to have had happened. But, one thing ruining your day would be a lack of emotional and mental control. Unless of course it was a serious event like the death of a family member. But, by saying to yourself, that you had a bad event and the rest of the day was fine, puts you in control of your emotions and your daily outcomes."

Kiera smiled and Megan tried to wrap her brain around it. "I guess I'm too emotional then." She laughed.

"It's alright. There is nothing wrong with being emotional. But there are people who want more control of their emotions, and this is one way to work on it." Kiera mentioned. "I can give you some books later if you want."

"What was your grant for, Kiera?" I inquired.

"A study of the descendants of the Amami and Yaeyama people of what was the Ryukyu Kingdom, and how Japanese Imperialism and western influences have erased their traditional practices."

"Did anybody understand that?" I queried the group and received a collective chuckle. Kiera shook her head and sighed, slightly annoyed. "No, seriously, I don't understand what you said in its entirety, but it still sounds cool."

“Thanks Tara,” Kiera smiled pensively. “I’m studying fading traditional practices in Okinawa and Japan.”

“That I understand. Sounds amazing! Did they give you a reason why they rejected your grant?”

“Someone else’s proposal beat me out for it, simple as that.”

“Still sucks.” Robbie responded.

“Yes, it does.” Kiera sighed in agreement. They clicked their beer bottles together in a halfhearted toast.

“I’m sorry honey. I wish I had known.” Robbie assuaged as he took Kiera’s hand into his gentle grip and gazed at her in a way of communicating like lovers do, that it would all be alright.

“Don’t worry about it. I plan to file a request to see the grant that beat out mine so I can study it and write a better proposal. Also, I asked several board members where I can improve to increase my chances.”

“Wouldn’t that be considered a conflict of interests?” I asked.

“It would if I went to the board members that denied my proposal. I asked other departments to review it and give insight into ways of improving, thus keeping me out of hot water.”

“Good for you!” Megan cheered.

“Alright everyone! How are you doing?” A familiar voice chirped over the microphone. I turned to see Peter on a small stage awash in the spotlight introducing the games of the night. He stood there in light gray slacks, and suspenders over a white dress shirt with the sleeves rolled up. The top two buttons of his shirt were undone, showcasing a tattoo that lay beneath. "It's good to see you all again. It's also nice to see some new faces in the crowd. Welcome!"

I waved at him, and Peter returned the gesture before getting down to the rules of the game. Our group enjoyed a night of frivolity, laughs, drinks and music. Kiera and Megan chatted while I got to know Collin a bit. Robbie enjoyed himself and between rounds of trivia would chat with Peter and other tables of players.

The night grew long and my energy was officially gone. After trivia was over, I went up to Peter to talk briefly about what else he did besides work in real estate and host game nights.

"That's about it. I don't get a lot of free time, but I enjoy the atmosphere here. Besides, hosting this isn't much different than selling real estate. You have to stay positive and upbeat but I get to be much more informal here which is good. It's a way to have fun and do something that I enjoy which is interacting with people."

"Okay. Well, it was nice to see you again."

"Same to you. Hope to see you back here for more trivia."

"You betcha!" I gave him finger guns as I backed away. Not sure why.

Stumbling back to the table I informed my friends that I was heading out. I was tipsy, I'll admit it, but I wanted to make sure Laika got fed before too long.

"Are you going to be alright getting home?" Robbie asked.

"I should be fine."

"Should be?" Megan asked.

"Yeah. I should be fine. I plan on leaving my car here and walking anyway. We aren't far from the terminal and it's a short walk to my house from the other one."

"How many fingers am I holding up?" Collin asked switching the number of digits between guesses.

"Three, two, five, three, one." I blurted with confidence.

"I will make sure you get home safely," Collin stated. "I never held up those numbers. I only held up four." He turned and wished everyone a good evening, and let Megan know that he would catch up with her later on after getting me home safely.

Collin stood and hooked his arm around me escorting me out the door and down the road. We talked along the way about how much we enjoyed the night. I asked him question after question in rapid succession as the alcohol I ingested flushed my face, burned my cheeks with heat and slurred my words. I wanted to know where he came from, how he knew Megan, if he lived here now, what he did for a living. Did he have a family? Married with kids? Did he always look hot, or was he one of those ugly ducklings?

Chances are I already asked all of these questions before, but I can't recall because my head is swimming.

Oh god, please don't think I'm an alcoholic or something! I hardly ever get this plastered.

With each question Collin smiled and laughed but answered them honestly even though I may not remember them tomorrow. As we boarded the ferry, he found a couple of seats for us, then went to the little shop on board to get coffee and a croissant to help soak up some of the alcohol in my system and stymy me awake long enough to get home. The coffee was absolute garbage. It was too bitter. I ate the pastry and laid my head on his shoulder.

"You smell nice," I whispered. He did. It must have been his cologne. I was picking up scents of moss, cedar and orange.

"Thanks," he grinned. I moaned in response and closed my eyes to rest. Keeping his position, he rested his head on mine and whispered as I drifted in the stupor between alertness and sleep, "You smell nice too."

The horn on the ferry was jostling. I think Collin asked if I was alright. I couldn't make out his words anymore, I just nodded and grumbled. With his help we headed to the top deck to disembark. I stumbled and tripped over my own two feet trying to guide him along the dark path to my house. Once there, I opened the door and Laika came barking at the new guest.

"Don't worry, she does this to everyone."

"It's alright. You said she needed to be fed, right?"

"Yes. Her food is in there," I mentioned gesturing vaguely to the kitchen before falling backwards over the couch and nearly falling asleep again.

"Right," he said.

"Should we get you something to eat?" Collin asked the dog. "You hungry?"

Laika twisted her head and barked when she heard a word she understood.

"Come on then." Collin called as they took to the kitchen and Laika led the way to her food. Collin fed her. My eyes closed, and the last thing I heard was the door closing.

CHAPTER 3

The next morning, I woke up with a headache. Laika was snoring on the floor right next to the couch where I had passed out. I sat up. My hair hurt. Soon I realized that it was pushed up at weird angles from sleeping in funny positions. I shuffled my feet softly across the floor and into the kitchen. I stumbled around a bit, still not entirely sober nor awake and brewed another pot of coffee.

As I shuffled off towards the shower, I noticed a piece of paper on the counter and stared at it. I moved it back and forth, squinting my eyes, trying to get the words to focus. Gah! This was difficult, but my lips pulled upwards into a smile as I set the note down and continued on my way.

'Glad to have gotten you home safely. I would love to get together for coffee and get to know one another a bit better if you're up for it. – Collin.'

I chose to get dressed in something simple and practical for putting the studio together, as I began working. I also packed a second outfit for after work, just in case. Laika made sure I didn't forget her breakfast, and then I unlocked her dog door so she was free to roam, and the two of us went about our days. For me, the first stop was Megan's house.

Moving up the road, I knocked on the bright red door. It swung open and Megan greeted me with a smile, coffee cup in hand.

"Good morning! How did you sleep?"

"Like a log. I never even made it to bed. I passed out on the couch," I laughed. "I wanted to stop by and say sorry if I did anything embarrassing last night and see if you would pass along my thanks to Collin for getting me home."

"I wouldn't worry about that too much. You didn't do anything embarrassing. I will make sure to tell Collin you said hi once he gets out of the shower, or you can tell him yourself if you want to wait a few minutes."

"He's here?"

"Oh yeah. He's staying with me until he can find a place of his own."

Without noticing, I moved forward before stopping myself. "No. I need to get to work setting up my gallery and studio. But if you could pass along my thanks, and let him know that I would love to grab a coffee later if he still wants to."

"Of course." Megan said.

"I am going to get going, I need to catch the boat across the way."

"I need to get moving too. I will see you later, okay?" Megan said as I stepped away from the door.

"Sure thing."

I took off, crossing Elliott Bay again and made my way down the street to find the car. It had been parked near the bar, and was still all right. It just had a few fliers under the windshield wiper. I tossed them in the trash, slipped into the vehicle and drove to work.

The better part of the day, I dedicated to arranging the workspaces. I set up a desk and hooked up the computer and design tablet, decided on a section for storing backdrops as well as C-stands. Studio lighting was erected and tested, as well as the studio strobes, my horseshoe mounted flashes, cameras and lenses. A cage was outfitted to the side with shelving where I could store the travel kit, light modifiers, camera lenses, camera bodies, rolls of film, ink cartridges, printer paper, as well as dark room supplies, poster boards, rag boards, fiber and matte print papers and extra bulbs. It was to remain locked at all times unless I needed to get something from it.

The next task was to set up a station where I could print large images, cut boards and press prints. Lastly, was setting up the darkroom in an adjacent space. Before realizing it, the sun was low on the horizon again and the day was drawing to a close. Locking up, I drove home and heaved a sigh of relief. Laika greeted me in the driveway, her tail wagging so much, the whole back half of her body swayed. The two of us sat out on the back porch overlooking the water until darkness enveloped us and I could see the stars and the scenic Seattle skyline.

I slept soundly that night. My motivation the following morning to find new subjects and locations took over, so I drove around scouting out spots with the camera, taking pictures and writing notes for later.

Before long, the weekend arrived, and I had made a date with Collin. We grabbed coffee and walked through the Japanese gardens. Later in the evening, we had dinner together and laughed over a bottle of wine before ending the day.

"I've had a great time," Collin smiled.

"I did too."

"So, would you like to get together again sometime?"

I bit my lip while contemplating and then spoke gently to him. "I would, but I have to be honest with you. I recently went through a bad breakup and I'm not really looking to get back into the dating scene. If you were okay with us just hanging out together as friends, then yes."

"I know," he mentioned somberly. "Megan told me. I completely understand and respect that. Honestly, I'm not much for the dating scene myself. I would rather have things progress naturally, if they do. And if they don't, then they don't."

I smiled and nodded becoming more confident as I understood what he was saying. "Yeah…yeah."

"What are you doing tomorrow?" He asked.

"Tomorrow, I will be out. I have to go scout out a photo shoot location near Deception Pass, so I'll be gone all day."

"No problem. Just let me know when you want to meet again, okay?"

"Absolutely. Thanks, Collin."

He waved to me as he stepped back from the door to return home. "Have a good night."

"Goodnight," I whispered as I closed the door.

The following day I put Laika in the car and drove to Deception Point National Park and let her run free for a bit while I snapped pictures left and right, searching for the perfect spots for a photo shoot. The day out in the fresh air proved beneficial and relaxing, plus I got a great spot picked out to work on.

By the time that Autumn had rolled around, I finally settled into a new routine. I had my work, I had Laika and I had my friends. There was an afternoon in the middle of October, I closed up my studio early and met Kiera at the university campus. She was done administering mid-term exams and graciously joined me for coffee at The Quad, before heading over to the Tateuchi East Asia Library to talk.

"How have you been doing?" I asked her.

"Oh, you know, living." She laughed half-heartedly.

"I can understand that. It must be rough to be a teacher here and still trying to advance your own learning potential."

Her dark eyes met mine at an angle since her head hung low. With an exasperated sigh, she shook her head in disbelief.

"How do you do that?" she asked.

"What?"

"See through people the way you do." She stared at me. "It's fascinating the way you can read me like any number of books on these shelves, and yet, you do so in a way that is neither invasive nor malicious."

It was my turn to laugh half-heartedly.

"Um, I guess it's learned behavior." I took a sip of my latte. "Can I be honest with you?"

"Of course," she brushed her raven hair away from her face, showing concern for what I may say next.

"When I was younger, I spent a lot of time living with my mom and sisters. My dad was prominent, but he wasn't always there. Even though I was the youngest of my siblings, I found myself in this weird position of looking out for them constantly. And that meant learning to read people's body language so that I could find out if they were potentially going to hurt one of us."

"That must have been rough."

"Yeah," I said dismissively. "It was, don't get me wrong, but what was difficult was getting it wrong, and watching someone I cared about get hurt, because I let the wrong person get too close. You know? I never learned to forgive myself for those mistakes."

"How old were you when you started doing this?"

"I think I was about eight or nine." Taking another small drink, I continued. "Needless to say, I've had plenty of practice watching people. I've been able to hone in on certain aspects of people, discerning personalities, seeing through the bullshit, et cetera."

Kiera laughed. "Must be nice. It's a good trait to have."

"Mm," I mumbled. "If only it worked on me."

"What do you mean?"

"It's the whole reason why I moved here. I let the wrong ones get too close. Some more than once because I was too trusting, or because I convinced myself to be trusting when I shouldn't have. I'm not entirely sure, even after all this time." I shook my head dismissing the thoughts. "I had to start fresh, recenter, refocus, whatever you want to call it. Which leads me to being here with you today at this beautiful library."

"Well, sort of," she stood up from a chair and escorted me around and outside the library. "I didn't ask you to join me so that I could show you this library. I'm actually going to introduce you to someone."

After a brief walk down a path, we came to an art gallery where Kiera introduced me to one of her colleagues who happens to work in the art department and helps with curating the gallery.

With a brief introduction out of the way, she pulled me aside. "Look, I know that you and I didn't exactly get off on the best of feet. I'm abrasive, and I tend to keep people at a safe distance. I'm a high-strung individual who cares about my career and accomplishments more so than most things. I recognize that in myself, but that doesn't mean that I don't care about my friends.

I can't make your pitch for you, but Robbie told me about your art gallery and wanting to get outside help from the university. So, I pulled some strings, and I'm putting you in touch with them. The rest is up to you."

"Kiera, I don't know what to say."

"Don't say anything to me. You need to speak to her," she responded, pointing at her friend. "I'll talk to you next week at trivia, alright? Right now, I have mid-terms to grade with my TA."

She left without so much as another word, waving and smiling. I was stunned, and her friend from the university could tell. A sheepish laugh came out, as I was completely unprepared to give a sales pitch, but here we are.

Several hours passed as we conversed and walked through the gallery talking about past experiences, relating to art in various forms and discussing business practices at large, as well as my background and business practices. I gave a rundown of what I was looking to accomplish, and what would be given to students in exchange, assuming that something could be worked out. Of course there were all kinds of legal paperwork that would need to be signed off, to include an approval by the Dean of the Department and the President of the university, but it was seen as a good venture idea for the students to expand on their knowledge since some may wish to open studios of their own.

I spent the majority of the winter months going back and forth with the school to get all of my ducks in a row for approval.

Kiera and I began to bond over some of the idiosyncrasies of the college and how things were operated. We met for coffee a few times when I was there to talk to the department heads. Otherwise, we'd do shots at the bar on Wednesday's and play trivia, catching up there. That was the only time I could recall her cutting loose. Robbie felt like we were sharing inside jokes. In a way, we were. But it wasn't to make him feel left out, it was just finally coming to some common ground with Kiera, despite her standoffish nature and high anxiety.

I bonded with Megan, based on her purity and good heartedness. She showed the best qualities that humanity had to offer, always willing to help out and listen despite her busy schedule, and I cherished that every single day with her. Somehow she managed her work on Tillicum, her personal life and somehow made every effort to join me at least once a week for dinner. She was a confidante and closer friend to me than anyone ever was before. I was skeptical of how easy it was for me to open up to her sometimes, but I tried to tell myself, that that was the trauma talking, trying to keep people at bay again.

With Robbie, we had a shared connection of architecture, and our little rivalry over whether it was construction or restoration. I wasn't going to let it go. Ever. And even though he got irritated sometimes, I know he liked it. I became like a little sister to him, I could tell by the way he looked at me and treated me. We got to bond every week at The Blarney Stone. Robbie was good with his hands and saved me lots of money on home repairs from time to time, always ready with a quick tip.

Collin was pleasant, but he maintained distance. He never pushed, but I could tell that he really liked me. I was smitten with him too and that scared me. I hadn't recovered, and trusting was only surface level for me right now. Throughout the winter we went on several coffee and museum dates. We talked about life, and without pressuring me, he would make sure I made it home safe at night, help me take care of Laika and be on his way again.

Spring rolled around and life picked up its tempo. With the snow melting, flowers blooming and birds returning to the woods, life brightened. Every opportunity I had to get outdoors, I took. I went to shows, walked in gardens and forests, hiked mountain trails and built a network of reliable friends who joined me on expeditions, or would come sit around the fire pit with me and Laika, drinking wine and staring out across the bay as we discussed life. Collin and I started to get a little more serious, and he would spend the night from time to time. Nothing sexual happened, but having him there helped me to start to feel safe around men again. I opened up more and we shared our first kiss on a ferry ride one night staring at the lit up Ferris Wheel on the pier as we travelled back across Elliot Bay.

I was on the top deck, just looking out, watching the waves and the lights, admiring what my life had become. I was content. He came up behind me and put an arm around my waist, pulling me closer. Melting into him, I lay my head on his shoulder.

"You doing alright?" He asked.

"Yeah, I'm fine."

"What are you thinking about out here?"

"Stuff," I replied.

"Stuff, huh?" He chided. "Good stuff, bad stuff, or just stuff, stuff?"

I could feel his body shake with laughter. Mine did too, as I wrapped both my arms around him and turned into his embrace. I looked up into his beautiful, caring eyes that sparkled in the dying light of the day.

"I was thinking about how fortunate I've been. How lucky I am to have the people I do in my life," I paused as without thinking about it, I lifted myself onto my tip toes and pressed my lips to his. They were full, powerful, and soft. He didn't force it, but just feeling our skin on each other in that moment was enough. I broke away, planting my feet on the ground again. "Stuff like that."

Without hesitation, he leaned down and kissed me again, and we enjoyed each other's company well into the night.

Over the next year, I began to build up my business. I created a steady stream of modeling clients, as well as contracting for businesses who needed employee headshots. I worked out a deal with the local university and college to allow several students to intern for a semester in order to gain valuable studio work experience in exchange for academic credit. Every Wednesday night I joined Robbie, Megan, Kiera and Collin at Trivia Night with Peter at The Blarney Stone. Things were starting to look up.

After trivia was over with, Collin would escort me back home and help out with keeping Laika company. Over this time, we had grown close without forcing it. We fell asleep one night on the couch with me resting in his arms. The next morning I woke up to a missed call on the phone. The weird thing is, I didn't recognize the number, but I knew the area code all too well – San Francisco.

No one left a message. I decided to view this missed call as someone from the past trying to get in touch with me again. I wasn't going to be baited into returning it. I deleted it from the log and went about my way, as today was a big day – Collin and I decided that we were ready to take our relationship further. He was going to be moving in with me, and I had a professional model shoot atop the bridge at Deception Pass.

I got ready for the morning and as I came downstairs, the smell of coffee tickled my nose, but it wasn't just regular coffee. Collin had this habit of brewing coffee with a dash of cinnamon to help with circulation and a little bit of kosher salt to cut through the bitterness of the beans. Toasted bagels made my mouth water, and the sight of Collin made my heart skip a beat. His light brown and blonde hair was cut neatly, his broad shoulders and muscly arms stretched the fabric of his henley shirt, tapering down at the waist to a nice, tight…you get the idea. He was stacked! I gave him a kiss as I reached for a coffee cup.

"Hey, good morning." He kissed me. "Are you ready for today's shoot?"

"Yeah, I think so. It'll be a long day, but I'm ready for it."

"Good. I'll make sure to take care of Laika tonight. I am going to head back to my apartment later and finish packing my things up."

"Sounds like a plan. I will see you later then," I replied as I finished my coffee and scrambled out the door.

A few hours later, I arrived at Deception Pass State Park with a caravan of workers, students and models in tow. It took three additional vehicles to carry all crew members, lighting and camera equipment as well as clothing, make-up artist and hairstylist. I had to work with a park ranger showing the required documentation for permission to set up and photograph in the park which took months to get approved. Together with the ranger, we worked out a spot where I could set up the tent needed for people to work and relax that was safe and didn't hinder traffic. A couple more hours later, the models and I were atop the bridge with several other individuals creating art.

Once the shoot was completed, the models changed back into their regular clothes. My assistants took down and boxed all the equipment and the tent. The stylist and make-up artist boxed all their gear, and in about an hour, everyone was ready to head back home. I gave the spare office key to one of the interns so that they can drop off the equipment at the studio, finish any work they needed for class using our gear and then lock up. I needed to hang back for a minute and clear everything with the park ranger before heading home.

After the final documents were signed, and I was cleared to leave by the ranger for not damaging anything, I was ready to book it out of there. It had already gotten darker than I would have liked. The sun had dipped below the horizon and the sky turned dark blue and gray. The air chilled, and the evening fog began to roll in again, not my favorite driving conditions. I was going to have to take my time getting back, meaning I was going to be super late. I sent Collin a text letting him know that I was on my way though.

I drove cautiously across the bridge back to mainland Washington. The only way into and out of Deception Pass from our location was over this stretch of road, about a hundred feet above the freezing cold waters of the Pacific Northwest. As I drove back down towards Seattle, a car with no headlights on came speeding across the bridge through the fog driving down the center of the road, not in their respective lane. I swerved on the bridge, slamming on the brakes and screamed out, "Jesus Christ! What the fuck!" My heart pounded as I scraped against the railing, but I gained control of the vehicle and continued on my way home fuming at the audacity and sheer stupidity of others. Now I needed to file a damn insurance claim. Fantastic!

That night when I got home, I snuck inside quietly. Collin had left the door unlocked for me. Laika was on the couch snoring, but woke up and growled when she heard me. I tried to console her, but she darted out her dog door to the back yard. Sighing in annoyance, I dropped my stuff on the counter and muttered, "Whatever."

She would come back of her own accord, she always did. I made my way up to bed, but paused momentarily on the steps for a ringing in my ears. I shook it off, getting more and more irritated by the inconveniences of the night.

Collin was sleeping already. Looking at him, so peaceful washed all of that away. A smile crept across my lips and I stole my way into the sheets, joining him. It had been a long day. I was sore, cold and tired.

CHAPTER 4

When morning arrived, I sprawled out among the sheets, stretching as I woke. Collin was gone. I was alone and opened my eyes to another hazy morning in the indigo inspired room. Dark and turbulent blue and white pillows nestled my head, and I removed myself from satin sheets to shower and prepare for the day. Down in the living room, a large art piece hung on the wall that had brush strokes of the vibrant color along with steel and gold tones. Collin was nowhere to be found, and Laika was out in the yard. I could only speculate that he had made some decorative changes last night while I was away, and was too tired to notice when I got back.

I went outside to get Laika, but she never responded. Upset, I crouched down and tried to move closer to grab her collar, but she dodged me and ran off. This was perplexing. She had never behaved like this before.

"Laika! Come!"

She continued to be disobedient. I tried running off after her when I spotted Collin. "Hey, Laika is running away. Can you help me?"

"Don't worry, I will get her. I think she's trying to play."

"Are you sure about that?"

"Yeah, we were doing it yesterday for a bit, while you were gone."

"Oh."

"How'd your shoot go by the way?"

"Not bad. I need to file an insurance claim before I forget and get back to the studio to work on the edits, do you mind if I leave Laika to you?"

"Yeah, no problem."

"Thank you."

"Insurance claim for what?" he asked.

"Oh, it's nothing. Just a scratch on my car. By the way, I like the decorating you did!" I called out as I took off for the ferry to the mainland.

Collin just waved back and walked leisurely in the direction of where the dog took off. I made my way down the road, swiped my ferry pass, boarded and headed inside for warmth. I opened the internet on my phone using wi-fi onboard to fill out my insurance information online. Now, I'll have to wait to hear back before I can get the damage to my car fixed.

On the other side of the Sound, I looked for a coffee shop and tried to check the news on my phone. There must have been some heavy cloud cover, because I was getting a very weak signal. Resigning, I put it away and enjoyed my drink. The sounds of people conversing was loud, and I tried to drown it out and turn my focus elsewhere. As I sipped, two figures walked by the window giving me pause. One was a young black man with dangling earrings, a leather jacket and vibrant colored shorts with high top sneakers. The other was a Korean woman in her early twenties with ripped jeans and an oversized sweater.

I couldn't help but think that there was no way those two would be here. If they were, it would be impossible for them to know I was here…hopefully. As I stared out the window after them, I realized something unsettling. The coffee shop was deafeningly quiet. Turning, I noticed that every patron and employee was staring at me. Each face was emotionless. A chill ran down my spine. Without realizing it, I had stood from my stool and backed into a corner. Every eye remained glued to me. Averting my gaze, I looked to see that those outside the window had stopped and turned to face me as well.

"What the hell is wrong with you all?"

***

"What are they going to do? Fire me?" Alonzo quipped in his signature sassy voice. "These people know exactly how long it takes to fill this position. And they know not to play around with my money. So, until they come to their senses!" he spoke louder. "I'm going to sit my black ass right here and keep doing what I've always done. My job!"

Alonzo had a dangling earring of a cross on the left and two studs in his right ear lobe. Aside from that, he had a short flat top haircut with shaved designs on the side and colored contacts. As he sat down at his desk in his jeans and sneakers, he rolled up the sleeves of his shirt up, and pumped lotion into his hand from the bottle he kept situated near the computer monitor.

"You are too much," Rina laughed.

"What did I miss?" I questioned coming closer, looking at the two of them before fiddling with my camera settings.

"Oh, you know, just Alonzo having a day," Rina responded between laughs.

Alonzo rolled his eyes, shaking his head and rubbed the lotion into his hands and arms.

"Girl, these people keep getting on my last gay nerve."

Rina doubled over.

"What happened?" I asked again.

"Oh nothing," he said calmly before exploding in a boisterous voice. "Just Mike trying to use my skills to his advantage without compensating me for the extra workload!"

His eyes rolled and he continued to moisturize his skin. "I'm not sure what it is about the air in here, but it keeps drying my skin out, and I don't want to be ashy."

He held the bottle out to me.

"I'm not ashy. Just pasty." I countered.

"You can be both," he replied staring at my hands.

"Bitch!" I quipped with an incredulous smile as I grabbed the bottle of shea butter from him and set my camera down. Alonzo took the camera from me to hold.

"You love me," he said as he turned to Rina. "I can't believe the gall of that man." He passed my camera to her and she continued to adjust settings on it before passing it back to me as I finished applying lotion.

"He's middle management," Rina assuaged. "He's only doing what someone else tells him to do. Don't take it too personally."

Rina was Korean. She enjoyed wearing oversized shirts. Her hair was cut in a bob that framed her round, porcelain face, and preferred to mix jewel tones and muted colors into a wardrobe that made her stand out amongst the others. She drew attention to herself, but refused to acknowledge it, making her seem off putting despite her sincere demeanor.

Alonzo on the other hand, was a firecracker through and through. He had no problem dressing loudly, speaking loudly, living loudly. From a conversation we had when we first became friends, he spent enough of his youth and early adult life dulling his brilliance for others. Now they are just going to have to shield their eyes if they couldn't handle his shine.

"So, get this," he said as he turned his chair towards me, leaning forward as if to tell me a big secret. Rina and I both leaned against the cubicle wall. "I was finishing up the campaign accessory layout for Kentaro, right? He's supposed to be here in a couple days, so I wanted to make sure everything was set before he arrived. Then Mike strolls up with that greasy ass combover of his, and says, 'Hey Alonzo. Could I get your help with something?' And you know me, I'm fine with being a team player, so I ask, what's up."

"Okay," I say with interest.

"He wants me to take on the Chaps account for their Fall and Winter shoots."

My eyes widened with surprise. Rina covers her mouth with her sweater. Trying to stifle her laugh.

"That's a huge deal!" I smiled.

"Oh, I know!" Alonzo said. "Do remember the debacle from last year?"

"Oh yeah," I recalled.

Last year, a major clothing brand had used our agency to head its campaign imagery. The downside was that someone within our agency had taken it upon themselves to add their individual flare to a massive corporate campaign that ended up costing our company millions of dollars having to reshoot and edit within a time crunch because it needed to be done for the next season's release immediately. Alonzo did a lot of the work behind the scenes to make sure that everything went off without a hitch. However, there was a downside to this. He didn't receive a bonus for the campaigns' success, only the team lead–who happened to be Mike.

“So now, Chaps wants to use us again. Cool. Mike wants to use me again because I made him look good. I’m glad he recognizes talent when he sees it. But I ask for a slice of the pie on the back end for my efforts and what do I get? Crickets!”

“I see,” I said nodding. “What did you tell him?”

Rina laughed again. “His exact words were, ‘Fuck you! Pay me!’”

“I’m not wrong!” Alonzo said defensively. “You want talent, pay for talent. Otherwise, you will get exactly what you pay me for–the bare fucking minimum.”

I shook my head smiling, “You are too much sometimes.”

He scoffed and rolled his eyes at me one more time. “Only to those who can’t get on my level.”

I put the camera up to my eye. Alonzo and Rina struck poses. I adjusted the focus and snapped their portraits.

After I dropped the camera to my side, Rina turned to Alonzo.

“If you don’t want to deal with the Chaps account, I’ll do it.”

Alonzo remained steadfast and put his headphones on as he turned to his computer, “I won’t touch it at all until I’m compensated for it.”

“Hey Mike!” Rina called as she walked off. “Can I talk to you for a second?”

***

My eyes squeezed shut. I whispered to myself that I was only hallucinating, it was a bad dream. The noise of the coffee shop filtered back into my ears as someone placed a hand on my shoulder and squeezed by me, apologizing for the intrusion. I assured them it was alright as I made my way to the counter, ordered a second lavender honey latte to go, and waited far away from the door and windows.

My heart sped up. I felt anxious and flustered as the blood pulsed in my fingertips. My mind raced, void of coherent thoughts. What were the odds of them showing up here? I never even told Robyn where I was headed for her own safety from Diego, and even now, I felt that security I spent the last year building as it began to crumble. If these two were here and found out, it would be likely that he could find out too. That is not something that I could let happen. I wasn't about to go back down that road of despair.

"Latte for Tara!" the barista called out.

My reverie was broken by those words. I grabbed the drink while smiling and darted out of the door. Carefully I made my way to work, keeping an eye out for those two on every corner I crossed. Arriving at the studio, I stole away inside, slamming the door and breathing heavily. I wasn't sure if I even took a single breath on the way here. It didn't feel like it.

My two of the studio aides, Vihaan and Lesya saw me as the wreck I was and greeted me, asking if I was alright. I couldn't speak at first. I just shook my head. "I don't know. I'm not sure."

"What's wrong?" Vihaan, one of the interns asked.

"I saw some people. I *think* I saw some people that I used to know. I hope it wasn't them."

"Were they horrible to you or something?"

"No. Nothing like that. We were old friends. I just haven't spoken to them since I moved here, and I don't want them to know I live here. It's a long story."

"Is there anything we can do?"

"Not regarding that, no, but thank you."

Vihaan and Lesya were cousins who were both trying to open their own business in art. Lesya was the older of the two by a year, but Vihaan was the more outspoken and authoritative of the two. The two of them got along at work, but still argued and joked like siblings would, at every opportunity. Having them around was lively for sure, but their work ethic was phenomenal.

"Have you guys gotten the photos uploaded on the drives?" I asked, changing the subject.

"Yes. We've catalogued it with keywords and made sure to fill in all the additional information on the metadata. They are ready for you to review."

"Excellent. We will go through them together in about thirty minutes, after I've had some time to compose myself."

"Sure thing." Both assistants walked away and prepared the computer and projector for the viewing. They set out notepads to write on and enjoyed their free time.

I set my coffee down for a second, taking a look to see that there was a sticker applied to my cup. A sun with a nightcap on it that said, 'wake up'. I smiled briefly and drank my latte before heading to the restroom to splash my face and compose myself. Looking in the mirror, I felt foolish and ashamed. I had gotten so worked up, that I even got the interns concerned. As a leader, that was not acceptable and was not something that I was comfortable with. I wanted to have an open and professional relationship with the student interns, but had to draw the line at what had happened because it was getting into the realm of personal. I needed to apologize to them.

"Okay, first of all," I said as I met them at the briefing table. "I owe you an apology for my behavior this morning. I know it was probably alarming, and unexpected. I need to give you some background information about me, since you are interning under me. For your own safety and understanding, I moved here a little over a year ago without telling anyone where I was going, not even my family.

I was in a horrible relationship with a narcissist. He was exceptionally controlling as well as emotionally, physically and psychologically abusive. It took me years to get out of it, but I did. The two people I thought I saw today were old friends of mine, but they were friends of his as well. When I cut ties with everyone back in San Francisco, I was hoping to never run into anyone again so I could remain safe and sane. I have trust issues stemming from him, and I can't trust that my old friends wouldn't tell him where I was, so I am avoiding them, if it was them. Forgive me for that kind of behavior, but understand that I do not intend to see or speak to anyone from my past."

The interns understood where I was coming from and thanked me for being honest with them. After we finished discussing that issue, they started their critique and conversation of the images.

It took over several hours to go through all of the shots. They criticized whether an image was too light or too dark, out of focus, too shallow or not shallow enough in the depth of field, and decided on a color tone theme for correcting them. After that, it came down to deciding the best of the best images in order to promote the story we were creating and if any needed to be composited.

"Alright, so I will leave you guys to it. Start with the compositing, get that out of the way first since it will take the most time. Afterwards, let me see how they turned out and we can turn our attention to retouching, and lastly, we can work on color toning and sharpening."

They left the table and went to their respective workstations. Vihaan and Lesya put on headphones as they worked, and I stepped outside the door and checked my phone again. Still no service, but I had one missed call from an unknown caller.

Luckily, with the wi-fi, I received an update on my claim with directions for what to do next.

Outside I photographed the damage to my car. I sent everything to the insurance company and an hour later, I had an email telling me where I could drop my car off for repairs and that they'd have a rental for me to cover the next fifteen days. Two and a half hours later, I was back to work.

The rest of the workday had gone by without so much as a hiccup, and a lot of work was completed. Saving our progress and shutting down everything, I locked up and thanked the students for their hard work today. They left with a wave of their hand, and I got in the car and sighed heavily, releasing the stress from my body.

I was tired; correction, I was exhausted. My mind had been racing all day on thoughts I wish I never had. Tension grew within me stiffening my neck and shoulders. As I got closer to home, I could see the lights on. The home stood out against the dark grey of the island and blue of the water. The indigo furniture accents and wall hangings stood vibrantly in the warm white lamp light. Honestly, it wasn't a bad design choice. It wasn't entirely my aesthetic, but not a bad choice. Collin had left a note that he had taken Laika for a walk and would be back in a bit.

Having the house to myself, I decided to draw a bath. The water gushed and filled the tub as I poured in some aroma therapy salts and lit candles. I was just about to dip my toes into the hot water when the doorbell rang. Collin must have forgotten his key.

Slipping my robe back on, I made my way downstairs. Behind the door was a surprise, as it wasn't Collin, but Alonzo and Rina, the two people I thought I saw this morning outside the coffee shop and wished I hadn't.

"Alonzo! Rina! Wow!" I stammered out in dumbfounded amazement. "What…what are you guys doing here? How are you doing?"

"We're good," Alonzo snapped.

"How did you find me?" I asked tensely.

"Can we come in? It's kind of cold out here." Alonzo pushed his way by me without waiting for a reply.

"Yeah, of course."

I stepped back, letting them in, offering them something to drink.

"That would be great," Rina replied. "Do you have any wine?"

"Always. You know me." I smiled. "Red or white?"

"I'm not picky, just whatever you have open is fine." She replied.

I grabbed a couple glasses, filling them and then excused myself to get dressed. I let them know that I was just getting ready to unwind when they arrived. Running upstairs, I threw on a pair of jeans and a sweater. Before heading back downstairs, I took a couple of ragged breaths, hyperventilating, followed by some deep breaths, reaffirming to myself that I could do this. I could get through this night. I had a lot of questions, and I'm pretty sure they did too.

"Sorry to keep you waiting," I chirped out. "How have you guys been?"

"Ugh," Alonzo rolled his eyes. "It's been a while since we've seen or heard from you, and that's the first thing you ask us?"

"Alonzo, chill." Rina responded. "Sorry Tara, you know how he gets sometimes."

"Sometimes? I am always a firecracker."

"Well, you need to slow down and be nice. Anyway, we are doing fine Tara, thanks for asking. How are you?"

"I'm alright. A little shocked to see you guys here honestly."

"Same."

"What are you guys doing up here in Seattle?"

"I got an assignment from Levi's so I came out here to scout locations for a new campaign ad. Alonzo decided he wanted to take some time off, so he came up here with me.

Honestly, I was sure I saw you this morning at a coffee shop, but we didn't have time to stop and see. When I had a moment, I checked online to see if your name popped up anywhere, and I found your studio. We drove by after location scouting and saw you headed home, so we followed you. I hope that's alright. Sorry to stalk you like that."

"Yeah! Totally!" I nodded while lying through my teeth. "Honestly, I wasn't sure if I saw you this morning or not when I was getting my coffee on the way in to work. I'm glad that I was right, and I wasn't just imagining things."

"So, miss thing…" Alonzo interjected. "Why didn't you tell us?"

"Tell you what?"

"Anything! You left us high and dry in San Francisco. No goodbye, no party, no forwarding address. You changed your number and dipped the fuck out. Care to explain yourself?"

"I needed to get out, Alonzo," I sighed. "I didn't do it intentionally to hurt either of you or anyone else, but I needed to leave Diego and his influence on my life behind for good. Unfortunately, that meant everything had to go, including my friends."

"But why?" Rina asked.

"Because he is too damn charismatic and persuasive and you know that."

"True," Alonzo nodded. "Remember that first night we met at one of his friends' parties and he tried convincing us all to do blow for the first time?"

Tara confirmed, "God that was such a horrible night!"

"What?" Rina asked. "It looked like you were having a good time."

"I was drunk on vodka and out of my mind. Then on top of that, I was pressured by my own boyfriend to snort powder in room full of strangers and almost immediately after, started tweaking out."

"You started dancing with everyone," Alonzo corrected. "And then you started to get undressed and make out with Diego and a few of his friends in front of everyone like no one else was there."

"Exactly! That was so humiliating for me. To have to be coaxed back into my own clothes like a child that doesn't want to get dressed for school. No. That is not who I am or who I want to be. I shouldn't have done that in front of a bunch of strangers, including you guys."

"That's how we became friends though," Rina interrupted.

"Not really, that's how you got to know about that aspect of me. We met and became friends because we worked for the same company."

"No, no," Alonzo shook his head. "We became friends because we finally saw you cut loose and realized there was a person inside that stuck up body of yours."

Rina and Alonzo both laughed. I shook my head and smiled defensively. "I wasn't stuck up."

"Gurl! You were more rigid than a mannequin! And you had just as much personality too."

"Wow, Alonzo, don't hold back on my account. Honestly, was I that bad?"

"No, I just have a flair for the dramatic. Look, we only met you a few years back because of work and you weren't the most fun to be around. You were too rigid, too professional. You didn't want to let anyone near you. We couldn't tell if it was a 'better than' attitude or if you were just introverted. We became friends because of Diego and his friends throwing that after party. Doing drugs wasn't the reason, it was seeing beneath the surface of what you projected that made us like you."

"Yeah, the few times we have ever hung out outside of work, were at his parties. And I hate to be a downer, but it was always exhausting to me," I remarked.

"We know, but you tried and it showed us that you cared to try for the sake of others which is what drew us to you more. We thought you would try to make things work with him and continue to be there for us." Rina said sadly.

"That's unfair." I couldn't help but feel my blood start to boil and I clenched my teeth and fists until I started to shake just thinking about it. "I couldn't put myself through that mess continuously just for you guys. I love you, I do, but the problems I had with him, I couldn't put up with anymore. I never saw you guys try things my way - staying down tempo and just hang out and relax for my benefit."

"That isn't our style and you know that. So instead of trying, you just leave without saying goodbye?" Alonzo snapped.

"Stop it," Rina said. "Look Tara, we didn't come here to fight. Honestly, I'm not sure if us coming over was a good idea or not, but I wanted to try and see about catching up since it had been some time since we've seen or heard from each other."

"It's been over a year now." Alonzo noted.

"I know," I said staring daggers at him. "To be honest, I would like to hear about you guys and what you have been up to first. Let me just order some pizza. And promise me, no more talk of Diego and his parties."

Food arrived and we continued to drink wine and converse. Alonzo and Rina had both been promoted within their company. Rina was promoted to Lead Location Designer. Alonzo is now in charge of compiling garment pieces for photo shoots. Both were very happy with their new roles and responsibilities.

I tried probing into their love lives. Rina had no one to mention, and Alonzo was sticking to being a serial bachelor. Then they turned the question on me.

"There is. Initially, I didn't want a relationship with anyone, I just needed to be alone and find my own peace. A few months after moving here, a friend introduced me to this great guy Collin, who has become more of a real partner to me in the past few months. It's not totally serious, but it is getting there."

"That's cool. What does he look like? What does he do? Is he hot? Come on girl, give us the details!" Alonzo coerced.

Something about the way he asked those questions tugged at my stomach. A sickly feeling like I shouldn't be talking about Collin to either of them because they may just turn around and tell Diego. His words hissing in my ear like a snake. Then again, I wasn't sure it wasn't entirely the fault of so many glasses of wine. I opened up a little about Collin, but used vagaries when replying. He was in his mid-thirties and very cute. He was retired from the military and building his own business working with his hands. He likes dogs and helps take care of Laika from time to time.

"When can we meet this mystery man of yours?" Rina asked.

"I'm not entirely sure. He should have been back by now, but I guess something happened."

I checked my phone again. Still no signal. Sometimes living there was exceptionally annoying with its lack of cell service.

"Well, I am sure that everything is alright. He probably just got held up because Laika found a scent to track and the fog is starting to get denser."

Rina whipped her head around to look. "Oh yikes! We should be going! We need to get back to our hotel."

"Are you sure you guys don't want to just stay here for the night? I can always make up my guest room for you?"

"Thank you," Alonzo stated, "but that's alright. We really should be going so that we can finish putting together our ideas for the next shoot. Rina must present it at the end of the week."

"Oh, well, alright. Thank you both for coming by. Look, I really am sorry about being so distant, but I really did miss you guys and am glad that we could catch up."

"Not a problem," Rina smiled as she exchanged a goodbye hug, "maybe we can meet up the next time we are here."

"That would be great." I smiled, despite the lie.

"Ok, and I promise, we won't tell Diego we ran into you."

"Thank you."

"Yeah, yeah," Alonzo quipped while twisting his wrist in a circle towards himself, "bring it in. It was good to see you."

"You too Alonzo."

"Look, I know we don't exactly see eye to eye, but we really did miss you. I'm sorry we couldn't meet your new beau. Give him our regards."

"I will."

Slowly, he let go of the hug and slid his hand down my arm as he remarked in a sultry voice. "Now go upstairs, draw yourself a nice hot bath, relax, and hopefully, we will see you again soon."

There it is again! That hissing in his voice. What the hell is that?

"Hopefully." I smiled, hiding my concern. "Be safe getting back."

They waved goodbye and went about their way, being swallowed by the dense cold fog as they stepped away from the warm porch light.

The fog was worse than I had seen before, and it worried me for many reasons. I couldn't get through to Collin, Laika was nowhere to be found, and I wasn't sure either of those "friends" were being honest with me, but for some dumb reason, I was still concerned with their safety getting back to their everyday lives.

Slowly I ascended the stairs to redraw the bath with hot water. The extent of the day left me drained entirely. First, it was just mental fatigue from meandering thoughts, but then physical and emotional exhaustion from the interaction with Rina and Alonzo. The quick lack of energy made me falter and wobble. My vision blurred a bit like when your eyes begin to shut for sleep. My head was swimming and I wondered if the wine wasn't making things worse.

While the tub refilled, I carefully re-lit some candles and set some music to play. Back outside the room for a moment, I tried to call Collin only to get his voicemail.

"Hey, it's me again. I am getting a little worried because I haven't been able to get in touch with you today since I left. I am hoping you're safe and maybe you and Laika aren't lying in a ditch somewhere? Anyway, call me back, please? Love you."

I hung up the phone realizing that this was the first time I had ever said I loved Collin. It forced me to pause and think about whether it was my emotions or whether it was just a reflex to say based on past experiences and genuine concern. Will he smile hearing those words? I couldn't handle any more of these questions. It caused a headache.

Something told me to call Megan.

I had one bar for signal.

"Hello?" She answered after a few rings.

"Hey Megan, it's me Tara. I'm sorry to call you so late, but just out of curiosity, have you seen or heard from Collin and Laika?"

"Yes. Both are here and sleeping. He was going to come back over, but he saw that you had guests and didn't want to interrupt, so he asked to just stay here for a bit, and they fell asleep on the couch. The two of them really are adorable together. Especially when they're snoring in harmony."

"Oh, ok. That's good to know. It would explain why he hasn't answered my calls. Thank you for looking after them Megan."

"Of course! Do you want me to wake them and send them your way?"

"I'll leave that up to you."

"Then I say we let sleeping dogs lay. I'll be sure to send them home first thing in the morning."

"Thanks Megan. You truly are a great friend."

"Aww," she smiled, I could tell in her voice. "Thanks Tara. Glad I could help."

"Ok. I'll make this up to you, I promise. Talk tomorrow?"

"Sure."

"Ok, bye."

Relief. They were safe, and the house was mine for the rest of the night. I needed to relax in the tub and go to bed. Hopefully, I'd feel better after soaking and I could put this visit behind me.

The water sent a tingling sensation up my legs giving me goosebumps as I slowly lowered into the steaming pool. The bubbles on the surface separated, leaving a gap in the shape of me. I smoothed them back over and played with them in the candlelight. Soft music echoed throughout the room, and I laid my head back, relaxing. The last thing I could recall was closing my eyes, a slow sinking feeling and the sound and sensation of ice-cold water filling my ears and drowning all else out.

CHAPTER 5

I woke up freezing in the empty tub with a stiff neck, and a banger of a hangover. I couldn't believe that I actually fell asleep in the bathroom! Goosebumps covered my skin. Shivers ran down my spine. I stood and exited the tub, only to turn the water in the shower on and then step back under its warming spray.

Maybe I have a drinking problem. No, that can't be it. I only had three glasses last night. Maybe it was the tannins?

A familiar bark faintly penetrated the sound of the shower. My head spun around with excitement that both Collin and Laika were home. I finished up quickly and dried off before fetching clothes from the closet. As I turned to lay them on the bed, I stopped in surprise. The sheets were gold. Just yesterday they were a deep bluish-purple. Okay, is Collin playing a prank on me? Confused and wary, I dressed and headed downstairs. All of the decorations that were indigo were now gold – appliances, furnishings, wall art–all of it.

Could Collin have redecorated the whole house overnight or in the early morning in a new color scheme? No, that couldn't have been possible. It would have taken too long and caused too much noise. Besides, what would he have done with everything he put up yesterday?

I tried to convince myself that nothing had changed, that maybe I was mistaken about it being indigo, but it nagged at me.

Coffee was ready and Collin was at the stove making breakfast. “Hey, good morning,” he smiled.

I gave him a quick peck of a kiss and rubbed his chest pretending everything was alright. “Good morning. How did you guys sleep?”

“We did alright. Megan was gracious enough to let us sleep there last night. But we woke up shortly before sunrise and made our way home so we could surprise you with breakfast in bed.”

“That’s sweet of you, but I’m up now.”

“I see that.” He laughed. “Breakfast will be ready in just a couple minutes, and we can have a meal together before you head off to work.”

“Oh god, I forgot about work today. Let me send a message to my team to take their time coming in.”

“Got anything big planned for work?”

“Um, yeah actually I do. We are going to be doing a fashion photo shoot on top of the Space Needle for a local designer this evening.”

“Wow! That sounds awesome. But how are you going to manage that with all the tourists?” He handed me a plate of pancakes, sausage and eggs.

“I got it cleared a couple weeks ago because I knew it would take forever to cut through the legal tape.” I sighed just thinking about all the hard work I had to put in. I continued. “Long story short, we got permission from an exec who worked at the corporation that oversaw the destination to allow us uninterrupted access to the top of the needle for three hours."

"Sounds amazing."

"Yeah, and what about you? You have any plans today?"

"I have a consulting gig today for a three-acre garden redesign in Port Gamble."

"Oooh, fancy!" I chided.

He smiled back. "I'm not so sure, but we'll see. I have my portfolio in the car ready to go. And if I land this one, then I may be able to land some follow-on work for my start-up business."

"Well, if you do, that would be awesome. Just make sure to thank Robbie later for the referral."

"Don't worry. I sent him a bottle of Scotch as a thank you gift. Hopefully, he likes it."

I stopped, "Robbie drinks scotch?"

Collin shrugged unknowingly.

The two of us finished breakfast and prepared for the day. "Hey Collin, I like what you did with the redesign here. I do like my all-white aesthetic, but these splashes of gold are pleasant too."

"Yeah, I heard you say something about that yesterday too."

"Well, you have a good eye for design."

"Thanks, but I didn't do it. I just assumed you did."

"What? No, that can't be."

"I swear, I didn't do it." He smiled, laughing half-heartedly. Something told me that he thought I was joking, and I wasn't.

"Neither did I."

"Then who did?"

"I'm not sure, and honestly, that terrifies me." I confessed.

"Same here." His brow furled. "I'll tell you what. I don't want you to worry about it. After my meeting, I will get some security cameras and install them so we can see what happens. I'll also get new locks put on the doors."

"Thank you," I reached out, gripping his hand. "I'll do my best not to focus on it. See you tonight."

Embracing him, feeling his warmth and feeling his chest move as my hand rested on it, I looked up into his eyes and kissed him gently, letting the feeling of his lips linger on mine.

"You should get going," he smiled.

"Sure thing. I will see you tonight."

I went about my usual habits on shoot days. I put headphones on and took my notebook out of my bag while riding on the ferry to review sketches and notes for the photo shoot. I jotted down additional notes in the margins about what aperture settings, light modifiers, and where to place things spatially.

I made a list of everything I would need and had it ready to go before the ship docked back in Seattle. I picked up my online coffee order before driving into work. When I arrived, I couldn't say that I was surprised to see some visitors waiting.

Oh joy! I thought facetiously.

Both Alonzo and Rina were leaning against the wall outside, drinking coffee and laughing. When they saw me, they smiled and waved. It was time to put on my brave face. I greeted them. "Hey guys! Good to see you again. How was the trip back last night?"

Alonzo said it wasn't that bad. The fog was thick, but it was kind of fun to get lost in it. Rina was irritated by how cold she got, because Alonzo wanted to take his time strolling to the hotel.

"Come on in, let me show you around my studio."

I swung the doors open and started to turn on the lights. I walked both old friends around the place pointing out the designated areas, and then we all had a seat in the lounge to talk while waiting for the rest of my team to show up.

"What do you guys think?"

"It's not bad for a start-up," Alonzo mused.

"Yeah," Rina agreed. "There are definitely some changes I'd make aesthetically, but this is still a great start."

"Thank you for being honest. I plan on making some updates in a while with Collin's help now that I have saved up enough money from working."

"How's your mystery man doing?" Alonzo asked.

"He's doing alright. He fell asleep at one of our friend's houses with Laika so he didn't show back up until this morning."

"Mhmm," he muttered.

"He has a presentation to give this morning for his landscape design company to land an account, then he'll be back home to do some work there."

"So can we swing by to meet him tonight?"

"Tonight is not a good night, because I am going to be on a photo shoot tonight. How about tomorrow?"

"We can do that," Rina thought aloud. "It's supposed to be our last day in town, but I think we can make it work."

"Can we tag along on your shoot tonight?" Alonzo asked. "Maybe we can help with costuming and lights?"

"Um, I do have interns that are supposed to do most of the work, but I can always use an extra hand with making a shoot magical."

Alonzo smiled widely. "Magical is what I do best. What's the shoot?"

"Well, if you can wait just a bit, I'll introduce you to my team and client and we can all go over it together before we start."

"Not a problem," Rina responded.

The three of us continued to gab. My phone rang, again with an unknown number from San Francisco. A part of me wanted to ask if Alonzo or Rina recognized it, but I wasn't sure I really wanted to open that can of worms right now. Instead, I ignored it and went back to conversing.

The rest of the team showed up an hour later, and they all sat in the conference room. I introduced Alonzo and Rina as well as the two interns, Vihaan–who everyone just called "V", and Lesya as well as today's models Terrence and Aliyah, along with the designer Frankie, and his hair and make-up crew. The entire group, all together, discussed the concept of the shoot for a local designer to promote his brand. The location and timing blocks of the shoot were discussed as well as the timing from start to finish with prep, travel, set up, tear down and unpacking. Everyone got to speak and give input on their specific areas of expertise and what they intended to do to make the shoot a success.

Alonzo had some ideas for styling the models that he wished to discuss with Frankie if he was willing to listen. Frankie was a little obstinate about collaborating at first. He had a distinct vision in mind, but I convinced him that having some help from individuals who work for a major fashion brand might help deliver a more concise vision for him in the photographs. Reluctantly, he agreed.

Rina sat back as I continued to go through the presentation and then opened the floor up to any additional questions, comments and concerns that anyone may have.

Both of the models had concerns about the locations that they were shooting at regarding safety, so I addressed them. I let them know that there is always some level of risk but that for some of their riskier shots, the tower safety and maintenance crew will be there as well as having the models wear harnesses to make sure they don't fall from any heights.

The interns took copious notes and gathered up the printouts of what I drafted this morning in my notebook. They got to work packing everything up in cases and checking them all off on their checklists.

After the meeting, I went back to my office to go through my email. Rina came in and leaned against the standing desk. "That was impressive."

I couldn't help but grin. "Thanks, Rina. I still get nervous having to do these meetings."

"You nailed it. I am actually really looking forward to helping out. But to be honest, I am kind of jealous that you got approval to shoot at the top of the Space Needle."

I turned my head slightly, wincing and I tried to shake it off.

There it was again–that hissing sound. What was that?

"Why?" I asked, ignoring the noise.

"I tried to get that approval process started yesterday, and they brushed me off."

"Ugh, I know what you mean. It took me over a week to get anyone to even hear my pitch."

"So how'd you do it?"

"To be honest, I flipped the fuck out. I was so tired of being brushed off, that I blew up, and then they finally told me who I should talk to."

"Too bad I didn't get to see that," Rina laughed. I laughed with her.

"Not my brightest moment, but it paid off."

"Any way you could help me get in contact with that person? It might make me look really good if I can get that permission for our account back home."

I took a moment to stop and look through the papers on my desk to see if there was anything there that would help, but I could not. I gave up and told Rina that I would just forward her the email. She hugged me with gratitude.

"Now, I need to get back to work, if that's alright. I want to make sure that everything goes smoothly tonight."

"Sure. I'll go find Alonzo and see if he wants to grab lunch. Want us to get you anything?"

"Yeah! I'm not picky, so anything you guys decide will be fine."

Alonzo and Rina dispersed. Time passed as I fluttered about the building making sure that all the tasks were going smoothly. I called ahead to the Space Needle reception desk to confirm that they were still good with allowing the shoot to happen tonight. Looking at the clock on the computer, I saw that it was just almost five p.m., a few hours before the shoot began, so it was time to get going.

"Alright everyone!" I clapped my hands to get their attention. "We have three hours before we start. It's time to pack up the gear and head over. Models, I need you in hair and make-up in fifteen. Frankie, you are with me. Alonzo and Rina, we will meet you at the tower. Lesya and V, you two have your completed checklists?"

They both held up their papers in response.

"Great! Let's get it all loaded up."

The three of us grabbed the gear from the locker and started putting it in the van. We had lights and reflectors, bounce cards, diffusers, black flags, extension cords and a generator just in case. Next was the camera equipment, stands, modifiers and the lenses as well as the colored gels and the completed permit paperwork for shooting on location in a folder for when we arrive.

Frankie climbed into the car with me. Lesya and Vihaan drove the van. Terrence and Aliyah left with the beauty crew and Alonzo and Rina seemed to have disappeared without a trace. Everyone met up at the tower and waited until I came back holding the forms folder over my head, waving for everyone to head up, and start.

It took several trips to bring it all in. It was also difficult to maneuver and manage everything because we were doing all of this while the crowds were still clearing out. I asked if Alonzo and Rina would be alright watching the gear up top while everyone else brought things in bit by bit. They didn't argue, and my crew worked diligently to get everything onto the elevators.

The tower visitors were curious as to what was going on and crowded around, forcing me to push my way through with the last bits of equipment. I huffed, annoyed with the ordeal, but still focused on the task at hand. I needed to work with security on taping off the workspaces or putting up ropes in the various areas as they moved about and getting those not working on the shoot back down to the ground floor, which many were dismayed with. I didn't care though. I had a job to do, and I didn't need someone jumping into my shoot "just because".

When the tower was quiet, I was able to help everyone set up their stations and the real work commenced. Luckily, we were only about fifteen minutes behind schedule, and the golden hour hadn't begun yet. I started the session with the top-down photographs by having the models lay on the rotating floor, and snapping shots whenever the ground outside became visible. Next, were the restaurant and lounge photographs in the golden light right before sunset.

Thanks to Alonzo's input in styling, Frankie was astounded by how the raw images looked and the storytelling of the photographs. Rina took some notes on her phone to take back and use at work herself. We were almost ready to wrap for the night. We just had one more set of photographs to get. Terrence and Aliyah went inside for their final outfit change. Lesya and Vihaan changed the lighting set up based off their notes and my direction. They took a few practice photos to make sure everything was right, while I was outfitted with a safety harness by the maintenance crew.

Once everyone was good to go, I explained what I needed the models to do. They were going to lean against the thick glass that surrounded the tower. These were going to be solo shots of them with Seattle at night in the background. Terrence was set up first and I started snapping his photos, posing him as I went. Aliyah was last. There were specific poses for her in mind, and I began to model what I needed her to do. The first was to lay against the glass with one arm above her head, the other, gently touching the glass, looking towards her reflection.

"Oh my god, this going to be such a beautiful story, Tara!" Rina said with excitement looking at the computer monitor. She stood behind the hood that blocked light from catching the screen at various angles and prevented glare. She looked at me and said, "I can't wait to see what other shots you finish up with tonight."

There is that fucking noise again!

I rubbed my ear, trying to clear any issues I was having. Hopefully, I wasn't developing tinnitus. It sounded not like a snake this time, but more like when air leaves a tire.

I turned back to the model and noticed a small hairline crack in the glass. Without panicking, I asked for a brief pause and asked Aliyah to take a breather. I went to a table where all my lenses were laid out. V came up to me.

"Did I get the lens wrong."

"No," I quietly replied. "Do me a favor and get me the maintenance chief, please and thank you."

The foreman arrived and I pulled him aside. "Not to be too concerning, but I saw that there was a crack in the glass that my model was leaning against. I'm sure that you will do a thorough inspection and replace it in a timely manner, but for now, I will need to move the set one more pane over, in order to shoot safely."

The man nodded and everyone got to work with moving. I called out to my teams. "Alright guys, sorry about that! We are going to make a slight adjustment to the angles and background. I just wasn't feeling it was conducive to our goals."

They all nodded and work commenced. When we were cleared in our harnesses again and the model was laying against a pane of glass without a fracture in it, I moved to the next adjacent pane to keep the distance necessary for framing. Before I put the camera to my face, I looked at Aliyah and contemplated. This was going to work. We are going to get an amazing shot! However, when framed through the viewfinder, it wasn't quite right. My shoulders moved so that I could get into a better position, but that didn't help. I needed to reset the way my whole body was angled. Pushing myself up and away from that panel, the pressure of forcing my body up caused the glass to shatter and I nearly plummeted to the street below. I wobbled trying to catch my balance and fell through the gap. I came to an abrupt halt dangling in the air from the harness and rope, screaming my head off for someone to pull me up. They worked to get me back safely and quickly, but the rope being pulled over broken glass split and I fell, my stomach somersaulting until everything went dark and I hit the pavement forcefully.

Or so I imagined.

I could feel my eyes wide with terror, unable to blink. My heart was racing and yet, I was still leaning against the glass posing the way I wanted Aliyah to. Internally, I screamed, *What the fuck?!*

Was that a premonition, a nightmare, or my imagination getting out of control? I had no clue, but I wasn't about to tempt fate and find out. Instead, I looked to Aliyah, smiled, and calmly said, "You know what, I have a better idea. Guys, can you please pull me back?"

The maintenance crew pulled me by the harness backwards and I quickly moved closer to the center of the tower. "I want to head back inside and finish this with a shot of you slightly away from the glass walls inside. If this goes like I think it will, it will allow us to have the city behind and beneath you, and if we can minimize the reflections, it will look like you're floating."

Frankie agreed to the concept and the crews worked on one last set-up. I looked at my watch to see the time. It was about eight-thirty. I could not get the weird hallucination out of my head; it was stuck on repeat. I ran thoughts by myself, thinking maybe I was tired or maybe some primitive part of me was warning me about heights. Maybe my conscience was trying to warn me not to do that photograph, or maybe I just went a little crazy. Regardless, the fear was real and my sweaty handprint on the glass was evidence to it. Nonetheless, I was going finish this shoot.

I congratulated everyone and thanked them all, on a job well done. I scheduled a day to review contact sheets with Frankie. Lesya and Vihaan took all of the supplies back to the studio. Alonzo and Rina went back to their hotel but thanked me for letting them tag along before leaving. I sat in my car, visibly shaking as tears poured down my cheeks and I cried aloud.

On the way back home, I tried to delve deep into my mind and get lost in thought. I was tired, so it felt easy to do and I drifted off before snapping out of it and jerking awake again on the ferry. I did this several times. I was now fearful I would fall asleep on the ferry and that something horrible would happen. In order to combat this, I moved to the upper deck and stood outside in the blistering cold wind as it howled, whipping hair about my face and pushing me back from the railing. Taking shelter on a bench below an overhang, I shivered in the cold night as the ferry sped across the water. At least I was awake.

When I finally arrived back home, the lights were off, save for a couple of lamps in the front room. Collin was already asleep and Laika was resting in her favorite spot. Quietly, I went to the bathroom to prepare for bed myself. I brushed my teeth and washed my face. As I reached for a towel to pat dry, someone handed it to me.

"Thanks," I muttered into the cloth. There was no reply. My eyes darted upward. In the mirror, I could have sworn I saw someone standing in the shower trying to bang on the glass. Whipping around, it was empty. My heart pumped wildly out of my chest as I slowly and carefully backed out of there and jumped into the bed pushing on Collin's shoulder to wake him up.

"Collin. Collin, wake up. There is something in the bathroom." I panicked as I eyed the darkened corner of the room. I couldn't get rid of that sense of being looked at.

He grumbled and rolled over, "Mm…what?"

"There is something or someone in the bathroom."

"What do you mean?"

"I saw this huge shadow in the shower, like there was someone in there watching me from the dark."

His eyes widened and he sat bolt upright. The bathroom door was right in front of us, closed tightly. Laika still snored in her bed. Collin put his feet on the floor gingerly and asked if I had seen anyone come in or go out.

Nope.

Carefully and silently walking to the door and slowly turning the handle, he open it. Reaching his hand inside, he turned on the light before opening the door entirely. He pushed it wide open, banging it against the wall. The noise startled Laika, and she began to bark ferociously. The hackles on her back went up, her ears pinned back, tail stuck out behind her, teeth bared. I had only ever seen Laika like that once before. It concerned me. Just the other day, Laika started barking at me, which was unusual, but even so, not like this. This was a sign of a frightened and terrified dog ready to protect herself and us.

Collin ignored her for the time being and stepped into the bathroom. The sink was fine, as was the bathtub. He looked at the stand-up shower stall. There was no sign of anyone in it. There was no sign of forced entry, or anyone escaping. He turned away from the shower, facing the mirror once more, he calmed his nerves and walked away.

Collin tried to soothe and reassure Laika, convincing her and me to go to sleep. He assured me there was nothing there, and it was all probably a manifestation of my sleep taking over before I was completely unconscious.

"You're probably right." I sighed.

"I know. Now, please honey, let's get some sleep."

He wrapped his arms around me and pulled me close to keep me warm and provide some security. I was too terrified to shut my eyes. They darted from the bedroom door, to the bathroom door, to the balcony.

There was no way I imagined something that horrifying, twice in one day. Did I? What the hell was going on with me?

Part of me wanted to cry. I was utterly terrified, but I didn't. I couldn't. Eventually exhaustion took over and my eyelids became too heavy to hold open. They drooped and my vision blurred as my eyes began to roll back in my head for sleep.

The last thing I remembered was another dark shadow lurking at the edge of the bed. It looked directly at me. Even shadowed, it looked familiar somehow. My body froze in horror. A tightness crushed my chest and I couldn't breathe. A stabbing pain pulsed down my left arm. I passed out.

CHAPTER 6

The next day I woke up and didn't move, frozen in bed. My eyes darted right and left. Collin was still there with me. I grasped his hand, and he returned my squeeze.

"Are you awake?" I asked without moving.

"Yeah," Collin whispered.

"Are you seeing this too?"

He cleared his throat and responded again. "Yeah."

"What color are you seeing?" I asked out of fear and curiosity.

"Orange."

"Same. You set up that camera system, right?"

"Mhm," he muttered.

"And how much data can it hold?"

"Twenty-four hours."

"Can we look at that now, please?" I cried.

"Yeah."

The two of us bolted out of bed, terrified and mystified. How did everything gold become a burnt orange hue? Even more concerning, how did the bed linens change colors with us still in them? What in the Amityville hell was going on?

We dressed quickly and ran downstairs. Collin grabbed his laptop and opened up the security program that he installed.

While we waited, I shakily made coffee, not that we needed it. Waking up in a newly designed room would startle anyone. However, I hoped that going through the motions of making and pouring drinks would calm me down and distract me from the terror welling up inside.

Collin let me know when everything was ready. I pushed into his side so that I could see the screen. We started the feed from the very beginning. Collin walked from room to room as he installed the cameras and then not a lot happened until he made dinner and played with Laika, then more time passed where nothing happened in any of the rooms. It was around nine-thirty on the timestamp that something happened.

"Go back!" I exclaimed.

Collin paused the feed. "Where?"

"There!" I shouted in fear. "Look at the art room!"

He clicked on the specific window that allowed him to enlarge any one monitor and view it. Once it took up the whole screen, I had him rewind the data a few minutes and then play it back.

We watched with bated breath, unable to turn away as we waited for something, anything, nothing to happen. My eyes fixed like a hawk to the screen, scanning and waiting. Then I saw that which made me jump in the first place. "There it is again!"

“What?” Collin asked as he rewound the footage another time and noticed it too. There was just the quickest of flickers in the screen. Normally, most people wouldn’t notice because if you blinked you would have missed it. It was quick, but I saw it. It shouldn’t have flickered. This was a brand-new system; I found it hard to believe that it was faulty.

“Is there any way to go frame by frame?” I inquired.

“Let me try.”

Collin tinkered with the controls and managed to slow down the video so we could view it with a more discerning eye. In that room beside my computer and next to a large format printer, an easel popped into frame with an image on it and then it disappeared again when the lights flickered.

No, that wasn’t the only disturbing thing. I looked at the wall. After the lights flickered, they changed color too.

With enough practice in photography, you can gain a certain level of knowledge and understanding in its science. One of those, most people don’t know, happens to be understanding color interpretations in black and white. You can’t see color in black and white, but you can see tonal variations and have an understanding of what the different shades and hues of gray translate to.

“There are two hundred and fifty-six different shades of gray, and in those two hundred and fifty-six shades, lies every color on the color spectrum. When a shade of gray starts to shift in luminance, then you can tell the color changed. That’s what the walls did. It was subtle, but their tone became more muted and darker," I explained to him.

This was a tell-tale sign. Still, something was off. How could that have happened in the blink of an eye with no one there to change it? And what the fuck was up with the painting appearing and disappearing on an easel?

Collin rewound the footage one more time and then let it play. There was the answer, in the bottom right-hand corner. The time stamp. It jumped ahead two hours while we were sleeping. We made a note to stay awake tonight during that time frame and see what was happening.

I marched Laika with me down to Megan's house to see if she could dog sit for a day or so. I didn't want her in the house with some ungodly occurrences going on. I had seen enough scary movies to know that demons won't spare dogs, and I didn't want to take any chances. When Megan asked me why we needed a dog sitter, I just told her that we were doing some interior renovations and needed to keep her out of the house for a bit. Megan understood all too well.

"I totally get it. I had to spend a couple days in a hotel not that long ago in order to have a mold/mildew abatement done. That stuff is toxic to breathe in."

"Yeah," was all I could think to say in response. "Thank you again, Megan. I'll make sure to pay you back for this."

"Tara, don't worry about it or this adorable furball. I kind of like having her around. You two have a good time, have fun with renovating, have a few glasses of wine, make a night of it."

Her voice became overly sweet towards the end of that statement. A chill ran down my back, but I was still happy she was helping me out.

I hugged her close. "Megan, I really couldn't have asked for a better friend. Thank you so much."

I went about the rest of the day trying my hardest to not be freaked out or concerned. Yet, the harder I tried not to think about something, the more it permeated my thoughts. Every time I tried to force my mind elsewhere as I worked through the day, I couldn't. I stood in the studio looking at the easels of artwork there, biting my fingernail, contemplating an orange image. Was this the one that popped up in my house?

I recalled the day I took that picture. It was at a local shoot in Sacramento. One of the models, Nika, was wearing this flowing yellow dress with a crown of flowers. I had her resting against a tree and holding a geometric object with fairy lights in it, to make her look like a fairy princess with a container of sprites. But the image before me did not show that. It was a negative, with all the corrections I made. It looked more like a skeleton draped in robes with a crown of thorns holding a mystical object staring not at me, but into me, ominously. I couldn't stand it.

I took the day off and sat somewhere to contemplate. I ended up on a on the cascading steps of the waterfront looking out over the water. Without realizing it, I was nervously biting my nails again. What was happening in that house? I looked up to see a portion of it from across the Sound sticking out amongst the pines.

It was early afternoon, I decided to go back home. I wanted to look around a bit. A voice in my head was trying to tell me not to do something so reckless, but another part of me needed answers, so I went.

Walking through my home on a normal day would seem inconsequential. Many times I reveled in the sunlight streaming in through the windows alighting the décor I kept minimalistic, allowing the home to appear decluttered and larger. Now, there is no comfort. Fear tickled the back of my neck, goosebumps covered me head to toe, chills undulated down my spine as blood pumped loudly in my ears and sweat formed and trickled on my brow as a pit opened up in my stomach.

Taking deep breaths, I moved from room to room. The bedrooms were alright, except for the crumpled sheets. Normally I make the bed after we get up, but not today. Hesitantly I viewed the bathroom where I remember the shadow from last night watching me. Nothing was visibly there.

I walked back downstairs to my art room where I occasionally worked at night and on weekends when I didn't want to be in my studio. There was a single easel in the room on the far side. It had an image on a purple background. It was a work in progress edit of myself for the ongoing project. I looked at it nervously from a distance. Megan's words popped into my head loudly. 'I get this feeling like I'm seeing something that isn't real. I mean, I know it's not, but it feels like it's of another realm, like what I would see in a nightmare. Not to say that it's terrifying in a bad way, but it looks like a human either emerging from or dissolving into this pool of color.'

Am I stuck in a bad dream that I just can't wake from? Why all of a sudden, did I get the sensation that the photographs were staring at me with malicious intent?

Averting my gaze, I gulped and moved over to my home computer turning it on and preparing it for later. This was the room where I noticed the changes first, so this is the room I wanted to be in. However, I was going to need some liquid courage.

To be honest, I wasn't surprised when the clerk looked at me as I was checking out asking if I was having a party since I had so much alcohol. I told her I was just stocking up for the next one, trying my best to put on a carefree smile.

She nodded in reply. "Cool."

Leaving the store and ordering a couple pizzas, I waited for Collin outside the house. Dusk was on the horizon, and I'll be damned if I stepped foot in there alone right now. It was almost an hour later that a set of headlights washed over me. I was relieved and stepped to greet him. It was not him though, it was the pizza delivery. Gladly, I took the food, thanked and tipped the driver before he was on his way; but I wasn't even hungry.

The smell could not entice me one bit. Minutes later Collin came home and was more than ecstatic about taking the food off my hands.

Back inside the house, we sat cuddled up on the couch just looking at one another for a bit. The tension in the air was thick and difficult to circumnavigate. I sighed heavily. Collin pierced me with his gaze and smiled. "You alright?"

I shook my head. There was no way in hell I was alright. Not even close. "Not really. I came back here alone earlier today because I couldn't focus on work."

"Why would you do that? I thought we agreed it wasn't safe to be here alone?"

"I know, but I couldn't help myself. I tried to stay at work and that didn't work; so, I went to the waterfront to relax and couldn't do that either. I don't know what got into me, but I felt it might be safer here in the daylight. I don't know why. But I ended up going to the store and came back waiting outside for you."

"Well, you're not dead, so that is a plus." He paused to look around and then locked eyes with me before continuing. "Try not to be so reckless again?"

"I'll do my best."

"Good," he responded as he leaned over to give me a kiss. Our lips touched and I felt his weight against me, his warmth encapsulating me, his aroma intoxicating me. I felt his arm reach over me, as if to embrace me, and then his hand retracted and he sat upright to eat the slice of pizza he grabbed.

I didn't know how to react to that. Shaking my head in disbelief I let out a small laugh before grabbing a slice for myself.

"How are we going to handle tonight?" he asked.

"Carefully. I want to stay in the art room tonight. I figured we could get some pillows and blankets, get comfortable on the floor and eat pizza and drink wine while watching movies until tomorrow."

"Alright, sounds like a plan. Any kind of movie you're in the mood for?"

"Something funny." I adamantly confirmed.

"Has there been anything even remotely funny released recently?" He asked, both bemused and skeptical.

"I don't know. I don't think so. I mean sure, there are movies listed as comedy, but what's considered funny anymore seems dumb."

"Yeah. Well, we'll find something, I'm sure."

We gathered all of the pillows off the bed and the couch, and created a circle on the floor that we could nestle into. Covering ourselves in blankets, we passed the time with food, drink and entertainment. Hours and minutes seemed to creep by when we got closer to the time last night that showed things changing in the room. Nervousness amped up inside me making my skin crawl like an army of ants beneath the surface. Anxiety twisted my stomach into knots, and I tried to drown it all out with alcohol. The next few hours were going to be difficult to confront.

Collin stood and stretched leaving me in the room alone to retrieve more snacks. I poured another glass of wine despite being well past drunk at this point. I should probably stop, but I wasn't ready to. I stood and stumbled about the room. I took in the sight of my artwork while inebriated, just to see if I felt any different about it. The thought of ghosts staring back gave me chills. The new one, the one of myself, haunted me the most. I scowled at it. "What are you staring at, ugly?"

I stumbled and knocked over an empty wine bottle. How many were there? Eight? I drank more. The image on the easel moved and blurred. I don't know, maybe not, I thought. I couldn't tell if maybe it was just my eyesight from the drinks. I tried to focus but couldn't. The room was spinning. My stomach churned and I dropped the wine glass. It shattered and I fell with it, smacking my head on the wood floor.

CHAPTER 7

Collin was patting my cheeks, shouting my name and shaking me. Laika was barking wildly and whimpering, doing what she could to make sure I was safe.

I couldn't see straight, not one thing I viewed held a definitive form. My body was covered in sweat, yet I felt the sting of the cold air. A metallic taste filled my mouth and nostrils. It was acrid and potent. I rolled onto my side and vomited. Apparently, this was not the first time I puked tonight.

Collin breathed a sigh of relief. After I finished expelling the bottles of wine I consumed, I coughed and tried to focus on him.

"Thank God! Take deep breaths," he instructed calmly. "I've got you."

My lungs rattled and rumbled. My limbs shook. Besides being cold, getting physically ill always left me weak and unable to support my own weight. It would pass in a few minutes. I just needed to get my mind in order. Laika came and started licking my face, so I focused on her muzzle as I tried to scratch behind her ears and let her know I was alright.

After composing myself again, Collin let me go and I stood on my own two feet. My vision cleared. I could see Collin standing next to me in the low light outside. The windows cast warm shadows across his face, and the look of concern caused me pause.

“I’m sorry.” I felt awful - both literally and figuratively. Not only did I get drunk, but so drunk I passed out, hurt myself, and caused Collin and Laika to freak out and take me away from the scene.

There was so much for me to unpack in that realization. One–Was I still bleeding from when I fell? The answer, yes, but not that bad. Apparently, when you slam your head into the ground on broken glass, you can cut yourself. Collin cleaned it up, but it was still bleeding a bit. Two–Laika licked me. Wasn’t she supposed to be with Megan? Where did she come from? Also, for days, Laika has been avoiding me and wouldn’t come near. I couldn’t figure out why, but today she needed to make sure I was safe? She cares, but that means there is something going on with Laika that she is dealing with too. Three–why did I have to be dragged outside? Collin couldn’t have taken care of me where I was? Four–what happened inside?

The last two questions required clarification, so I proposed them to Collin.

“I had to move you. I heard your glass break from the kitchen, and when you didn’t respond I came to check on you. You were face down on the floor, glass, wine and blood mixed together, and that’s when I saw you start to convulse. You were throwing up while unconscious, drowning in your own bile. I picked you up and rolled you onto your side, but that’s when I started to get dizzy.”

“Dizzy?” I interrupted.

"Yeah. I got lightheaded, and everything around me started to blur, so I did what needed to be done. I grabbed you under the arms and I dragged you out of the room and out the front door. I wasn't sure if it was a gas leak inside of the house or not, so I wanted to be safe. I called for Laika, and we have been out here ever since."

His last sentence was muffled by a hissing sound in my ear again.

"How long have I been out?"

"Not long. A few minutes, maybe ten at most."

"I have to see inside."

"Don't go back in there. I don't think it's safe."

I hate being told what to do, or not to do, but he was right. It wasn't safe inside if both of us suffered from dizziness in the same spot. I was just going to peek inside the window to see. I went back toward the art room where my image was and peered into the large glass opening.

I wish I could say what I saw surprised me, but it didn't. The interior changed again. This time it was a vibrant ruby color.

"Hey Collin, do remember what time it was when you got up to grab snacks?"

"Um, it was a little after nine, I guess. Why?"

"What time is it now?"

He looked at his watch and cleared his throat in an unsettled manner.

"What time is it, Collin?"

"Two. It's two in the morning."

I turned toward him knowing full-well that something ominous happened. Not only did I get blackout drunk, but ten minutes doesn't become five hours unless something insidious was at play. There was no way we could stay in the house again. I was going to need to talk to the realtor and let him know I needed to sell this place ASAP.

Looking around for a second made me pause. "Where's Laika?"

"She's over at Megan's, remember?"

"No, she was here with us. She was licking my face when I woke up."

"No, she wasn't honey. You may have been suffering from a mild hallucination, left over from waking back up."

"I wasn't hallucinating," I said vehemently. "She was here. I heard her barking, and she was licking my face. You said so yourself, you called for her and have been outside ever since."

"Honey, please. I am not trying to pick a fight with you. I believe that that is what you saw, felt and heard, but she wasn't here, nor has she been here. It was just the two of us all night. You dropped her off with Megan before work yesterday."

I couldn't help it. The tears stung as warm rivers flowed down my cheeks. What the hell was going on with me? Was Collin lying or playing some cruel, sick joke? Where was my dog? There was no controlling it. I sobbed until I slept again.

Chirping birds roused me gently. Collin held me in his arms, snoring lightly with his head craned back against the wall of our home. Peeling his arms off me gently, I stumbled around the yard a bit, barefoot and shivering. I wasn't about to go back into that damn place alone, again. Instead, I marched over to Megan's and rang her doorbell.

I heard a familiar bark from inside. She was here. Megan answered the door groggily. Her eyes were half closed and puffy, her hair disheveled, clothes crumpled. None of that mattered when she laid eyes on me. Her eyes widened and she pulled me inside. I immediately fell at her feet, crying yet again.

Honestly, I don't blame Megan for not knowing what to do. If I were in her shoes, I would have had the same problem. She did her best though. She helped me to my feet and took me to the kitchen. She made me coffee, grabbed a warm washcloth so I could clean up my face a bit, and then listened to me about my problem.

When all was said and done, she offered me some clothes to borrow and walked me back home with Laika at her side. We woke Collin, who was still sleeping soundly, and stood outside our house discussing last night.

"I'm sorry, I didn't tell you this before. I wasn't sure if you would believe me. Hell, I still have trouble believing myself."

"Yeah, totally," Megan muttered. "So should we go in together?"

"I really don't want to," I said apprehensively. "But I will."

Collin stood and dusted his clothes off, speaking assertively. "Yeah, let's do this."

Laika stayed outside on the porch and just laid down, refusing to budge as she licked her paws.

Inside the house, everything was eerily quiet and still. The lights continued to shine in every room from last night. The kitchen and art room were a mess. Blood and wine were dried, staining the floor in beautiful shades of macabre offset by glittering shards of glass. It matched the ruby dressings that adorned the house - the dressings that neither I nor Collin installed.

We moved from room to room as a group, never leaving each other's side. Hoping to find any clue to what was going on. Nothing was out of the ordinary, except everything was. We left the interior and scanned the outside of the house. Nothing was amiss.

Collin called the utilities company to see if there wasn't some kind of a gas leak in the house. They were sending someone over immediately to investigate. In the meantime, I needed to speak to Robbie and Shawn.

Megan and I both walked to his place. Laika followed at a distance. Kiera answered the door. She looked well put together, and gave us a look as if she was about to leave her house and had interrupted her.

"Let me guess, you need to speak to Rob?"

"Yes, please. If that's alright?" I asked.

"Sure. He's inside," she mentioned as she gestured over her shoulder. "But can you get out of my way please? I'm late for a meeting."

"Oh sorry, I didn't mean to…"

"Of course you didn't. You couldn't possibly have known."

"Is it for your grant?" I asked as she pushed by.

"Yes."

"Good luck!" I called after her.

"What's with her?" Megan asked.

"Don't worry about her. She's just trying to focus and get in the zone. She doesn't want to lose her research funding again. Remember how she lashed out last year?" Robbie answered. "Excuse me for a sec."

He moved past us to the car and knocked on the window. I watched as Kiera huffed and begrudgingly lowered it. Robbie stuck his head inside, whispered in her ear and gave her a kiss on the cheek. I could only imagine that it was words of encouragement because she relaxed, gripped his hand and kissed him back before driving away.

"Sorry about that, ladies. What can I help you with?"

"How much do you know about my house?"

"Excuse me?"

"How much do you know about my house?" I asked again.

"Are you talking about its architectural design and layout?"

"No. Do you know about its history."

"It's history? There isn't much history to it. I'm pretty sure that it was built twenty or so years ago. Wouldn't that be a question for the realtor that sold it to you?"

"What about the last person who lived there? They didn't happen to die there, did they?"

His brow scrunched in concern. His breathing paused as he tried to wrap his brain around the question, and what would bring about that question?

Pointedly, he responded, "No."

"Okay, thanks." I despondently sighed.

"Is everything alright?" He asked as Megan and I began to traipse away.

Megan looked back and shook her head. Robbie shouted for us to wait. He went to grab his shoes and jacket so he could join us. The three of us walked together back towards my house with

Megan on my right and Robbie on my left, staying close to me for assurance.

"Why are you barefoot?" He whispered to me as we walked back.

"Long story," I grumbled, shivering mildly.

When we returned to the house, Collin was still waiting for the utility truck to arrive. He too was barefoot, but he was all right in his long sleeve Henley and jeans. Robbie noticed this and asked him what was going on.

"Morning Robbie," Collin said. "We honestly don't know. Something weird is going on with our house. Last night, we lost a couple of hours of time and both of us had some dizzy spells. So right now, we are making sure we don't have a gas leak inside."

"Have you guys gone to a hospital at all to get your heads checked?" The wording of the question didn't go over well, and he realized the need to recant his query. "I'm not saying that you guys are crazy! I am just saying, if you can't account for some hours, maybe you need to make sure that whatever happened didn't cause any neurological problems."

I was embarrassed to answer this.

Do I tell him the truth? Should I just air out that the last few nights I feel like I have died and come back again in a redecorated home? Should I be honest and risk being seen as crazy? No, I wouldn't be. Even Collin has seen what is happening. We aren't suffering from shared psychosis.

I agreed. "You're right Robbie. Is there any way that you could take us, or call us an ambulance at least? My phone isn't getting any signal."

"Sure." Robbie reached for his phone and called for an ambulance. We waited as a group until they arrived and triaged the two of us. They said that everything seemed fine, but they would take us to the ER for additional testing anyway.

We agreed to go, but not until after the house was checked. Robbie disagreed with me. "You two need to go. I will wait here for the inspection and let you know. As soon as I have an answer, I will call you. I promise."

I wasn't sure what to do or think. He was right. I should go and get tests done, but I wanted to make sure there wasn't anything else going on. I didn't want to have a doctor tell me that I'm crazy. Also, what was I going to do with Laika? I looked at Megan, and she caught my worried eyes.

"Hey," she coddled. "Don't worry. I will take care of her. Robbie will manage the house. You two need to get some shoes, and get going. Let us know how everything goes."

Nodding and turning, Collin and I both took a deep breath in, rushed inside and grabbed the first pairs of shoes we could find and ran back out of the house before exhaling loudly. He helped me up into the large EMT truck and followed me. Together we went to the nearest hospital, which was St. Michael's in Silverdale.

Our visit consisted of neurology exams, psychological evaluations, coordination tests, blood tests and vision exams. It was an exorbitantly long day and I was weary of it all. I just wanted answers. Due to the uniqueness of the situation, Collin and I were treated separately to make sure there was no coercion in our recounting of events.

I was done first. I sat in the waiting area with a cup of coffee, unable to look up and meet the eyes of anyone. Eventually, my cup got cold, and then I began to drink it. That's when he came sighing and sat down next to me. He patted my thigh and told me everything would be alright. We waited for the doctors to call us back again. We closed our eyes from exhaustion.

I was tired and so glad it was time for bed. The fatigue was palpable. It had been a long day spent with friends, and my social battery was drained. I just wanted to crawl into the sheets. I lumbered to the bathroom, turned on the lights and brushed my teeth. Collin joined me. He talked about the day and how much fun he had while flossing. He was glad to get out of the house and spend time with people outside of work again. We shared a few laughs. It was good to explore the island with them, but now both his feet hurt. I agreed by muttering, "uh huh" from around my toothbrush.

After rinsing my mouth out and taking my evening pills, I washed my face. The menthol within the astringent left my skin refreshed, cool and tingling. Kissing Collin on the cheek, I left the bathroom and climbed between the sheets.

Removing the weight from my feet was satisfying. To feel the pressure released from my soles as I settled in caused me to reflexively let out a sigh of relief. My feet still throbbed, but at least they would calm down while I slept. The cold white linen caressed my skin, comforting and welcoming.

I pushed the pillows off the bed and nestled into my cocoon for the night. Collin was not far behind me. He turned off the lamp on the dresser. Only the ambient light from the small salt lamp cast a faint glow in the room. Shadows loomed around us, but it didn't matter. I was exhausted. My eyes were already closing. I felt the pressure on the bed change as he crawled in next to me. I drifted off to sleep.

It couldn't have been for long though, because I could feel something was off. I woke up, and he was gone. My arm shot over to my left, trying to feel for his presence. All I could feel was the mattress. I called out to him, but got no response. Just silence. A deafening, eerie silence. Not the kind you hear at night when everyone else is sleeping, but the kind that comes to mind when thinking of the world becoming void of all life. That kind of silence that only exists in death.

Where was he? I looked to the left, he wasn't there. I looked to the right and the bedroom door was still closed. The bathroom door ahead of me was cracked. Maybe he had to go again after drinking water before he fell sleep? I couldn't see the light on.

I called out. No response. Then I noticed that Laika was missing too. She always sleeps on her bed near the foot of our bed. I can normally see her if I crane my neck a little, but not this time. Something blocked my view.

At first, I couldn't tell it apart from anything else, but then I saw a glimmer, like the reflection of light in an animals eyes at night. That wasn't Laika. The figure grew, unfurling, standing, looming over the bed, sucking the light into its void of a form, encapsulating the room, touching the ceiling and bending forward towards me.

I was frozen in terror again. There was nowhere to run, nowhere to hide. I was stuck defenseless in this bed. The creature growled, rumbling the walls. Its arms slowly manifesting in the darkness, its talons sharp and deadly.

I let out a guttural noise. I knew this was the end of me, and I was afraid. The being moved from the foot of the bed, to right next to me faster than my eyes could comprehend, faster than I could react. With ferocity and speed, it grabbed my head and pulled. I screamed and flailed, fighting back uselessly against this thing.

I woke screaming, my arms thrashing, fighting my invisible assailant, but halfway sitting up in bed like I was being pulled up and out. The subtle light of the salt lamp cast shadows across the room. Laika lay in her bed snoring. Collin was still right next to me, fast asleep, unphased by my night terror. I was drenched in sweat, too traumatized to go close my eyes, stuck staring at the spot where that thing manifested itself, hoping it wasn't real. I prayed for daylight to come quickly, but also waited, mentally preparing for that thing to pop back up.

The hair on the back of my neck stood up. Even though I couldn't see anything, I could still feel its presence there. It was getting closer and closer to me. Stalking me in bed. I felt the pressure of a hand on my shoulder and screamed, shooting awake.

The doctor jumped back, startled. My heart raced, and Collin was spooked as well. I apologized for the outburst and explained that the stress I've been under caused me to have a bad dream.

The doctor pulled us into an examination room to talk to both of us. The tox screens came back negative, as well as the urinalysis and the CT scans. Our physical examinations showed no deficits, and our cognitive tests turned out fine. In all respects, we are a medical mystery, since there is nothing wrong with us. We were told to return immediately if we begin to experience any new or recurring symptoms, and then released with a prescription for anti-anxiety medication and told to follow up with our primary care providers.

None of this made sense. I could feel my sanity slipping away and the hysteria setting in. It started with a numbness – a mind void of any thought or capability to think, followed by weakness in my limbs. Slowly, but surely, I could begin to feel synapses firing and nerves coming back online. My legs wobbled, a heaviness invaded my gut, rocks in throat made it impossible to speak. What was I to do? What were we to do?

With a vacant expression, I held on to Collin and we left the hospital. The two of us sat outside while waiting on a ride back home. I didn't want to go there. He didn't either.

"We could go get a hotel room…?" he thought aloud.

Stuck in my own mind, I never heard him. Shaking my shoulder gently, he snapped me back to reality and asked me again.

"No. I don't want to spend the money. I have a boudoir shoot coming up, and I set it up at my studio. We could stay there."

This piqued his interest, and I could care less about that. Honestly, I was hoping that something holy remained within the walls of that studio left from its days as a church annex. Thoughts swarmed around me that something extremely sinister was going on, and any ethereal help would be welcomed at this time.

We arrived at the darkened studio, and I unlocked the doors. Quite honestly, I wasn't sure which was spookier to me, the creepy house that changed décor daily, or an old church at night that I was now using as a workspace. I began to think that maybe this wasn't the brightest of ideas. Then again, nothing felt like a good idea anymore. I questioned and doubted everything. Hopefully that will all stop soon.

Collin helped me turn on the lights and we settled in for the night. He ordered food for delivery while I set an alarm for the morning so we could both be up before anyone else arrived for the day. I checked my voicemail to see if anything came through from Robbie – nothing. Collin locked the doors to the building for safety and looked around. I just realized that he had never been to my studio before. I gave him the grand tour to help take my mind off things while waiting for food and sleep.

As I finished showing him around the locker a loud knock echoed. Sushi and tonkatsu arrived. He tipped the delivery guy and locked up again. I stayed as far away from the door as I could. I couldn't shake the unease of open doorways right now. I was reverting to a more Paleolithic mindset, of hiding in caves at night, closing it off to predators until daylight. But had we ever really come very far from that? The two of us nestled onto the bed I had set up for the shoot tomorrow. He held me close, trying to reassure me that everything was going to be all right. I didn't believe that for a second. Turning to gently kiss him on the cheek, I whispered, "You're lying, but thank you."

Staring intently, softly, I could see the range of emotion dancing across his eyes as he gazed my way. I smiled back meekly, unable to put on a façade of happiness.

"What is it?" He asked.

"It's nothing." I whispered, shaking my head.

"Now who's lying?" he smiled at me. "What is it? Tell me what you're thinking."

"It's these dreams I've been having lately. You know how sometimes if you have a bad dream, you wake up, but then it creeps back into the front of your mind again the next time you lay down?"

He nodded.

"That's what's happening to me. I am trying not to think about the things that my brain wants me to think about."

"Well, you know, our brain does that, not necessarily to scare us, but to confront that which is bothering us the most, right? So, as much as we don't like it, it may be best to think about it. I can help you, if you tell me?"

I didn't know what to say or think. I looked at him for a while, contemplating it, urging myself to just be up front and truthful, fighting that feeling that said he would think I was nuts, and blurt it out. "In my dream, I saw a monster or a–a demon, and it tried to kill me twice."

His eyebrows shot up, his head tilted and there was a slight nod before he said, "Well, alright." He ate some more sushi before continuing with a mouthful. "Were you able to see it, or was it just an unknown in the dream?"

"I could see it. It attacked me in the bedroom."

"Do you remember how?"

"Um…" I stammered, uneasy with recalling. "It kind of unfolded itself, and then used speed to reach me before trying to pull my head off."

Collin paused. "That's pretty graphic."

"You asked." I said shamefully. I could feel the tears on my cheeks again. Stress was overwhelming me. I sniffled as I wiped them away and went back to trying to eat.

Collin continued to watch me. His eyes were filled with concern and sympathy which was surprising to me. He and I were dealing with much of the same issue, but he didn't seem to be worried about himself. Just me. A sense of passion washed over me in the moment, and my love for him ignited. I placed a hand gently on his face, caressing his jawline. I stared into his eyes and kissed him. In that moment, all fear subsided. He wrapped his arms around me, enveloping me in his warmth. Tears continued to fall as my lips caressed his and our bodies mingled.

To say that the night was passionate, would be an understatement. We had desecrated every room and work area that night with our desire for one another. No surface was safe, and we knocked many things over that night while in the throes of our lovemaking. Not that either of us actually cared. When all was said and done, we settled in the bed, caressing each other softly as we locked gazes. The night grew longer, and sleep eventually took us.

At one point, I woke up coughing. The room was dark, so I reached for my phone, and then tried to make my way to the bathroom without waking Collin. He was still sound asleep. As I got into the adjacent room, I turned the light on and coughed repeatedly into the mirror. My head spun and stars danced across my vision. However, nothing seemed out of the ordinary. Splashing my face with some water and taking a few sips, I went back to the main area of the studio, and turned on a light. Hopefully, it wasn't too bright, but something was wrong and I needed to find it.

I scoured the area that we lay in, and as I looked, I got down on the floor. I took a deep breath in as I pressed my chest to the wood planks and had another coughing fit. This one did wake Collin.

"Tara! Are you okay? What's going on?"

"Oh god!" I choked out. "Something isn't right." I looked up at him to see that blood was spilling from his nose. "You have a nosebleed."

Collin wiped his hand across his face, smearing blood along the length of his index finger. It wouldn't stop flowing. He ran to get something to press against his nostrils. My eyes darted around, and then I got to my feet and headed for the darkroom. I had a suspicion and I hoped I was wrong. As I opened the door, I was knocked to my knees by an invisible wall. A wave of nausea swept over me and my eyesight went black, coming back in a blurred state. Forcing myself upwards, Collin rushed to my side and put a hand under my arm to help me. When I looked over, he was much worse than before. His skin was pale, and blood began to drip from his ears as foam formed at the corners of his mouth.

He was a horrid site to behold. What was happening to my beautiful man? Why was this nightmare persisting? Tears welled in my eyes yet again, and I sobbed, grief stricken and terrified. I needed to get him outside, before he died. Chances are that it wouldn't take much longer. Collin reached over to me, and put a wet paper towel to my face to cover my nose and mouth, cleaning up the blood that came from me.

Taking his arm, I turned and headed for the emergency exit next to the dark room. As we got closer, I reached out and turned the knob on the wall that was used to operate the industrial air circulation system, hoping it would circulate the air out and allow clean air in as we made our way outside. The door didn't open at first, but I heard the fan start up. A large mechanical whirring noise. But it shouldn't have been as loud as it was.

Collin and I pushed with our combined strength that we had on the door and it barely budged. Both he and I were much weaker than expected. Looking at him, I could only imagine how terrifying I must look. We leaned into the door. As we did, we heard a loud clunk. There was a metallic grinding sound and then a flash of light and intense heat that followed a loud bang. Fire spread across the floor of the studio. Without realizing it, Collin shielded my body with his as he pushed himself on top of me and against the door to open it. We both fell outside on the hard concrete as an explosion seared the skin off his back. He couldn't speak. His body just twitched and trembled, seizing, and I couldn't comprehend what was happening.

The fire kissed my skin and heat radiated up my legs as it gave me blisters. The weird part, was that I couldn't feel the pain. I think I was in shock.

Collin took the brunt of it all. I couldn't move and neither could he. I just looked up at him and locked eyes as the light in his faded. He was dying. Of this, I had no doubt.

"Colin, I'm…sorry. I love…"

He collapsed. Flames continue to lunge at my legs. Everything went dark.

CHAPTER 8

"Ma'am! Ma'am! Can you hear me?" A strange woman's voice called out. I couldn't see who it was. A fuzzy white orb pierced the darkness and I winced.

"Pupils are dilated and responsive," she called out in a hurried tone. "Ma'am, can you hear me? If you can, I need you to try and squeeze my fingers."

What is going on? Why is that voice so garbled? Why can't I see anything clearly? What happened? Where am I? Where is Collin?

"Where's Collin?" I croaked out.

My voice was hoarse and small, my speech slurred. Everything was spinning, making me nauseous. Turning to my side I vomited before everything went dark again.

"We're losing her!" Someone shouted.

Those were the last words I heard.

When I awoke, it was to the steady sound of a monitor beeping, and a woman in green scrubs checking vitals while taking notes. I stirred in the bed, and she ignored me, walking out of the room.

It was some time in the middle of the night when a woman in a lab coat came in. She pulled the curtain divider back. The rings made a noise that echoed in my ears, piercing in sound.

Then she did it again to give privacy to whomever was on the other side. My body shuddered.

"Hello, there. My name is Doctor Ahmadi. I'm glad to see that you're finally awake. Can you tell me your name?" The woman pulled out a pen light and shined it directly into my eyes.

"T, Tara," I stuttered. "Tara Musgrave."

"Good, Miss Musgrave," she cooed and clicked the light off. "Can you follow the tip of my pen for me please?"

She moved the pen in different directions and I followed to the best of my ability while she continued her questioning.

"Can you tell me what day it is?"

"Um…Tuesday, September 23rd? It might be Wednesday. I…I'm not entirely sure."

"Good." Doctor Ahmadi put the penlight away and looked at me.

She was strikingly pretty and young. She had hair like obsidian, and her eyes were speckled green. The more I looked at her, the harder it was to look away.

"You're very pretty," I admitted.

She blushed. "Thank you. Miss Musgrave, can you tell me what happened and why you're here?"

My brow furled as I tried to concentrate. Images flashed as I recalled the night. "Something woke me up. I was coughing a lot.

I tried to find what it was. I was at my studio and then this wave hit me."

"Wave? Can you describe it for me?" She scribbled on her notepad and checked my vitals on the machine behind me as I tried harder to recall.

"I don't know. I opened the door, and then there was just this invisible rush. I was lightheaded and my nose started bleeding. Collin was there too. He was bleeding also…is he alright?"

"Miss Musgrave, I need you to focus on events right now. I am unfamiliar with this Collin, but I can find out in a minute after we are done here. Please, tell me more about your incident," Doctor Ahmadi probed.

"Collin was bleeding. It was horrific." My eyes glazed over in a panic as the memory came to the forefront quickly and vividly. I envisioned his face before me. "Blood was flowing from his nose, his ears, and even his freaking eyes. He was foaming at the mouth. It was terrifying."

I paused, stuck in horror at the thought of it before I muttered, "I think there was a chemical spill in the darkroom. I tried to turn on the suction fan to clear the air…" I tried to shake the memory away. "It failed. Something backfired. The room went up in flames so fast. Everything was burning. We tried to escape. The door was jammed. He threw me against the exit and shielded me from the blast."

Doctor Ahmadi watched me closely as I recalled the events. "He died trying to protect me." There were no tears this time, just a stunned revelation. Collin was dead, and it was my fault. My lip trembled.

"Miss Musgrave," Doctor Ahmadi called. "I understand that you are in a very vulnerable state, and you have my condolences. However, my job right now is to treat you to the best of my ability. And I will do that. However, I need your assistance in doing so. Can you recall the chemicals you think were in that spill?"

I shook my head. "No. Not right now. I need some time for the fuzziness to wear off."

She nodded approvingly. "Of course. I will continue to have the nurses come in to monitor your vitals hourly, and I will check back after you have had the chance to get some more rest. In the meantime, is there anyone we can call for you? An emergency contact or family?"

"Collin was my emergency contact, but um, you can search my phone contacts for Megan. She's the only Megan listed in my phone, and she's dog-sitting for me. The code is ninety-two, ten."

Silence filled the room.

"Okay," Doctor Ahmadi stated awkwardly. "In that case, please do your best to rest. I will try to get in touch with her. Once again, I am very sorry for your loss."

She pulled the curtain back and forth again. The sound gave me a headache, grating my fried nerves. I lay there alone in the silence for a moment before I tried to get out of bed without unplugging anything. It wasn't easy. As I uncovered my legs, I saw the white gauze running the length of them. Same with my arms. Trembling, I held onto the railing as I got out of bed, moved the monitors, rolling them along next to me, using the metal bar to brace myself on the way to the bathroom. The fluorescent light made me cover my eyes. It was too bright. After adjusting, I looked in the mirror. My face was covered in gauze.

With trembling hands, I pulled on the wrap. With each layer removed, it turned darker shades of red until the bandages were stuck to my skin, soaked in crimson. My reflection was marred and grotesque. I must be in the burn ward. I puked in the sink, but nothing came out, just dry heaving. When I finished, I rewrapped the gauze as I fought back tears that wouldn't fall and returned to bed. This was a nightmare.

The nurse in green scrubs came back through again, checking my vitals. She still didn't make eye contact with me or say anything. She scribbled on a notepad and walked away, as silent as could be. I closed my eyes and let the pain medicine lull me to sleep.

I didn't have any dreams, so I guess I slept well. When I woke up, all I could see was the fluorescent lighting above. As my vision cleared, I was able to make out the chart on the wall with notes for the nurses. It said: morphine 8 mg/mL; 50 mg/12 hrs. Bandage change q 4 h prn. Toxicology pending.

The world passed by outside, and I stared at the ceiling contemplating what reality was for me, and if this was it, because it felt so unreal. The curtains were pulled back again. Doctor Ahmadi stood there and was surprised to see me sitting upright.

"Miss Musgrave. Good morning."

"Hi," I muttered, staring ahead.

"How are you feeling?"

I contemplated the question. "Awful. And I look like a monster."

"Tara. May I call you Tara?"

I nodded.

Doctor Ahmadi sighed. "I can understand that you may feel like a monster, because you have undergone a traumatic event that has left you visibly altered for now. However, with treatment, over time, we can correct the damage that has been done to leave minimal markings."

"That is a very robotic response," I sneered. "You're doing your job to the best of your ability. I see that. But don't bullshit me. Clearly, you can see, I'm not in the mood to be lied to."

Her posture straightened and she cleared her throat, recovering from the exchange. Before she could speak again, I cut her off.

"Hydroquinone and potassium bromide. Potassium ferricyanide, mixed with hydroquinone and potassium bromide." Doctor Ahmadi started scribbling frantically as I continued to list off chemical compounds. "Sodium thiosulfate, sodium sulfite and sodium bisulfate. Potassium aluminum sulfite and boric acid. Those are the chemicals you asked about."

Reviewing the information, she muttered to herself, "Severe chemical burns from a laboratory."

"Darkroom." I corrected. "They're the chemical compounds used to develop film negatives and prints in a photography dark room. Typically, I store them carefully. But Collin and I got wrapped up in our own intimacy that we ignored the mess we made. I know what the warning labels say on those bottles, and I know what happened. I've had years of training to prevent this very mistake."

"Can you elaborate?"

I nodded meagerly. I wasn't confessing to a crime, but to an accident. It didn't feel that way to me though. "Developer, fixer, stop bath, anti-fogger. All are steps required to preserve film and prints. However, the chemicals themselves are caustic. They can ruin your clothes, and if inhaled in concentrated quantities, have damaging side effects. The biggest problem is that you won't know until it's too late, because it's odorless, colorless, it's deadly and flammable. When certain compounds are mixed, they make sulfur dioxide. When heat is applied, they make hydrogen cyanide. And then it all combusts."

I whimpered morosely.

She stood stoically in front of me. "Tara, I'm going to take the information that you have given me and do a little more research. I want to make sure that we prevent any lasting tissue damage from this incident. There is more I would like to cover with you, but only when you are ready."

I blotted my eyes with a gauze wrapped hand and nodded, choking back the sobs.

She continued. "There was extensive damage to your face, arms and legs. Your midsection was remarkably untouched, which would account for what you said about being shielded. We have done a fair deal of debridement to your extremities. There is much more that needs to be done; however, it must be accomplished in phases to keep from causing you any additional pain. The next session is set for a little later today. Do you have any questions regarding this?"

Sniffling, "Is it going to hurt?"

She nodded slowly as she responded, "We will do everything in our control to reduce the pain, however, there will be some discomfort."

I continued to cry into the bandages, sobbing as I processed everything and tried to convince myself that I would overcome the challenges ahead and the pain, but right now I couldn't. Doctor Ahmadi sighed and continued.

"I am also required to tell you that now that you are awake, I had to inform the police. They are here to speak with you about what happened."

She stepped back and two officers entered the room to converse with me. Hours passed as we went over my history, what I was doing at the studio that night and my relationship with Collin. I recounted detail after detail multiple times, tiring of the inane questions. I was starting to get the feeling these two were trying to catch me in a lie, and it pissed me off.

"Why don't you two just come out and ask the damn question already! Did I start the fire and purposefully kill my boyfriend?" The two officers fidgeted uncomfortably. "No, I did not. And I won't tell you again that the fan backfired causing the spark. It was a horrible, fucking accident. All right? Now, if we're done here- "

One moved to speak and was stopped.

"No, they're done. Thank you, officers," a stern voice commanded.

I looked over to see Megan standing there with her arms crossed. She stared daggers at them, stepping back and holding her arm out to usher them from the room. The two uniformed individuals thanked me for my time as they left and Megan watched closely.

"Thank you," she called with false sincerity. Once the coast was clear, she turned to me in a panic. "Oh my god, Tara, are you okay?"

"No, I'm not fucking okay Megan. I'm in a goddamn burn ward!"

I bawled, becoming more and more emotional as the days continued. The stress I was under was too much to manage.

"What the hell happened? I got a call from a doctor that I was your emergency contact, and that kind of threw me."

"You were the next available contact."

Her usually bubbly demeanor waned, and her toothy smile was absent. "I…I don't understand," she said.

"Collin was my emergency contact," I paused as the lump in my throat returned and I forced a swallow, "but he died in the fire, trying to protect me."

Megan's legs gave out and she crumpled to the floor in disbelief. He was a great friend to her for years, so this loss would be devastating to her. She cried. I cried. We cried. A nurse came in again, the same one from earlier, who didn't speak. She was middle-aged and trim with her hair pulled back into a ponytail. She helped Megan into a chair next to the bed and checked my vitals once more. Then she turned to me and said, "Miss Musgrave, I hate to interrupt, but it's time we take you to your next appointment."

A team of individuals in the same green scrubs flooded the room and started moving equipment, unlocking wheels on the bed, opening the curtains and shuffling me off. I didn't have time to say goodbye to Megan or to apologize to her. I just yelled back, my voice breaking, "I'm sorry. Take care of Laika."

The next few hours were absolute torture. My body was alive with pain as my nerve endings were exposed and treated with water, my skin removed from my body, excised and flailed with scissors and I was wrapped again like a wet mummy. The medication wasn't enough to combat the pain, and discomfort was an understatement. I would have to talk to Doctor Ahmadi about her choice of words later. Right now, I needed to rest.

Given another heavy dose of medication to alleviate the pain as I was wheeled back in, Megan stopped pacing. She must've been there the whole time. I don't know how I deserved a friend like her.

In that moment though, she didn't look happy. She was biting her fingernails. Her eyes were piercing nothingness, lost in thought. She waited until we were alone again, and with a sigh, she dropped her hand.

"You know," she started with mist in her eyes. "If your face wasn't already fucked up, I would slap the shit out of you. Dammit Tara! How fucking dare you! How dare you kill *my friend*!"

Her hands curled into fists, and she swung them. I was terrified she might hit me. She needed to let that anger and despair out, but she refused. She fought that urge and I could see that it took everything in her to do so. I lay motionless and helpless. If she wanted to, she could have done it, and I wouldn't have been able to stop her. She had every right to feel that way.

She started pacing again faster each time she crossed the room before she abruptly stopped. "I don't know how to handle this, but I do know that I can't stand to look at you. Why I'm still here blows my mind. I-It's not, it's not like I owe you anything," she stammered. "I want to say, 'Fuck you and your dog!' You know that, right? I really do." She paced again. "I'm not that kind of person though. I'm better than that. I will be better than that. I like your dog," she said through tears. "I will keep her safe. But I don't envy you for one fucking second, Tara. I wish you a speedy recovery, because when you're free, you and I are through…I need to go."

Without hesitation, she left the room. I wasn't sure if she was saying those things because of the hurt and grief, or if she truly meant it. Not that it mattered. They still stung more than the wound treatment. I remained motionless.

What the actual fuck? Why can't I move right now? I can't even shed tears. What did they give me?

The sliding of the rings on the long rod echoed. The curtain was pulled back and away. Doctor Ahmadi stood there. I couldn't do anything but stare at her. I know her. Knew her? Her familiarity to someone I knew was uncanny. Where did I know her from? Everything was blurry again, my mind fuzzy.

"Nadihne?" I asked.

The curtain closed again, the rings echoing.

***

"Okay everyone! Thank you for coming out today! I'm excited to be doing this project, and I'm glad you were all willing to take part in this," I beamed with excitement.

Surrounding me were models, make-up artists and assistants to help things go off without a hitch. Over a dozen of us were crammed into a small studio space, music blared through a speaker somewhere and models clamored away with one another as they talked about their previous works.

I continued. "Everyone, please be sure to look over your model release forms carefully before you sign them! If you have any questions, let me know! I can work with those of you who are part of an agency hire, if any of the verbiage needs to be adjusted per your contracts. MUA's, make sure I get your contact information and social media tags so that you get credit for your portfolios!"

It felt like no one was listening, but it didn't matter. I'd grown to know that it is always chaos behind the scenes before shooting begins. The air of excitement permeated everyone before we got down to business and the bulbs began to flash.

I pushed through models that were changing clothes and providing critiques and updates to the make-up artists as they finalized looks. I saw one and stopped. She was stunning, and the make-up was all wrong. I stepped in.

"Absolutely not. This is not what was in the brief. Her make-up should be natural and complimentary to the beetle that was assigned to her for the shoot. Don't make her *look* like the beetle." The young model smiled. "She has a great complexion and skin tone. Her insect is this beautiful iridescent green. I need both of them to stand out."

The MUA was dumbfounded. I didn't want her to think I was stepping on her toes and shattering her creativity entirely. That's not how you made friends in this industry. "I love the look, don't get me wrong. I love it. But, how would you feel if we went with a complimentary color story as opposed to monochromatic?"

The aspiring MUA looked at the bug in the box on the workstation in front of her, then to the model and up to me.

"Um, I think that the complimentary color would be too jarring. What if we went analogous?"

My eyebrows shot straight up. "What did you have in mind?"

"Gold?"

"Is that a question or your response?" I queried.

"Gold," the woman said again more affirmatively.

"I love it!" I beamed into the mirror. "Here's what I'll do. I'll reorganize the model order to give you more time to refresh the look. Keep the same style to the makeup because it is stunning." Both the MUA and model looked at me in the mirror. We all gazed at one another. "I'm obsessed with your skin! Oh my god! It is so clear! I'm jealous."

Nadihne smiled sheepishly. "Thank you."

"No, thank you! It's an honor to work with stunning individuals such as yourself who aren't afraid of bugs."

"I grew up with brothers. It's nothing new for me," she shrugged.

"Fantastic," I replied. "I need to get going, I look forward to working with you soon…" I trailed off, waiting for her to introduce herself.

"Nadihne," she smiled. "Nadihne Ahmadi."

"It's a pleasure. I look forward to seeing you on set," I called as I made my way over to my assistants and started going over all the necessary paperwork before shooting.

The day flew by. Hours passed in mere moments and models loved working with the butterflies, beetles, dragonflies and other etymology that was provided. The MUAs would carefully touch up their looks as some began to sweat under the lights and my assistants were hard at work making sure I had what I needed, moved lights and blocked sets as necessary while also reviewing images to make certain that nothing was out of focus or framed improperly.

Nadihne was the last of the day. She was patient, timid and professional when it came to taking directions and making sure, we got the best images possible. Over the hour we spent together, chemistry ignited between us. She was my favorite model that day.

At the end, I thanked everyone for their time and dedication as I shoved the release forms into my case and packed up.

Nadihne hung back as everyone else cleared out.

I turned to her with concern. "Was there something you needed?"

"Not really. I just wanted to watch if that was alright? I'm new to modeling, and this is my first paid assignment. I want to learn everything that I can about the process and industry. I think it would help broaden my view of what goes into campaign work and make me more marketable later."

This was surprising. Models don't typically take the time to learn about behind the scenes work if it isn't relevant to them. Their focus stays on modeling workshops and the mirror so they can get poses and facial expressions right, which isn't surprising considering that some models will shoot two or three assignments in a day, or one with multiple looks. Nadihne however, was curious and that made her peculiar.

I crossed my arms and legs as I leaned on a table. "Well, what would you like to know right now?"

Her face was expressionless. "Anything and everything."

I asked how much time she had as I readjusted my posture.

"I have a few hours tonight, and then I can always coordinate more time later for more things if necessary."

What an odd answer. I didn't agree to show her anything yet, but she's acting like I already have.

"Okay," I hesitated. "Tonight, I'm going back to my work center and uploading files. If you want to tag along, you can. Otherwise, I have your information on the model release, and we can meet up another time."

"Like I said, I'm new and I want to learn as much as I can. I'll tag along, if you don't mind."

"Not at all," I said unenthusiastically.

We drove back down toward The Embarcadero. It wasn't the safest place at night, but at least I wasn't alone. The lights were on inside the studio when we arrived. Someone else was there late which was always suspicious.

"Hello?" I called out.

"Tara, is that you babe?" a voice called.

I sighed, turning to Nadihne with a smile. "It's just my boyfriend."

"Oh," she smiled.

"Diego, I'm just here to show one of the models how we catalog the pictures."

A Latin man appeared, muscled with tattoos on his hands, arms and neck, wearing a tightly fitted suit. His eyes were dark and smoldering with a heat of seduction. His smile was gentle but sly. He hugged and kissed me before greeting Nadihne.

"Welcome," he said before talking to me again. "I'm finishing up for the night. Will you lock up when you're done, or do you need me to stick around?"

"No, I got it. You go home and get some sleep. I'll see you soon."

We kissed and he left. I watched Nadihne watching him go. She must have taken a liking to him. How couldn't she? He had a magnetism about him that caused women to naturally gravitate.

"Anyway!" I spoke loudly to break the trance she was in staring at his backside. "Let me show you what we do after the shoots are complete."

I turned my back and rolled my eyes. Nadihne followed behind into a room of cubicles. The only difference from a typical cubical farm were the black boxes called hoods that covered the computers to keep the overhead lights off them.

"Industry standard," I said as I pointed at one. "It's hard to edit when your screen has a glare on it."

"Cool." She nodded.

We spent the next hour in the office cataloging images with keywords and downloading backups to external drives. It was boring and tedious, but now Nadihne was able to see the not-so-glamourous side of fashion and photography work. When we were ready to call it a night, I took her back to her car.

"That was eye opening. Thank you," she stated. "I know it was probably awkward having me tag along, but I appreciate it and the learning opportunity."

I nodded. "Not a problem. Get home safely, or your agency is going to wring my neck, alright? Someone from our team should reach out to your manager in a couple of days with edits. We'll talk more then."

Nadihne waved as I drove away.

"What an odd duck." I muttered, staring at her in the rearview.

***

Something startled me awake, my heart pounded in my ears with that revelation. The room was dimly lit, dusk creeped in, and I needed to get the hell out of here. Hurt or not, I wasn't sticking around to find out what was really going on, and why she was here pretending to be a doctor. I carefully turned the machines off and unhooked the monitors. I know they'd come quickly because someone should be monitoring vital signs somewhere on the floor. I was just going to have to risk it.

No one walked the halls. The silence was too quiet, and it left me unnerved and wary. I walked a liminal space and part of me hoped that I got caught by someone, anyone, so that I didn't feel alone. The emptiness was haunting, the silence deafening.

Footsteps echoed off the green walls, the setting sun casting a fiery glow in shrinking squares. I tried staying hidden, but it felt like the shadows would swallow me whole, so reluctantly, I was forced to stay in the pools of light as they diminished.

Behind the floor desk, a bag with my name on it was tucked away. My phone, keys and bloody and burnt clothes were inside. I also found a badge that had been dropped. It belonged to a woman in her later years, respectable and serious. I looked it over and saw the name. Doctor Nadihne Ahmadi. The face wasn't the same as the doctor treating me.

Clinging to the badge, I found a scrubs dispenser and put a couple of open-backed gowns in, to retrieve a clean set of scrubs to cover my bandages. There was no way to hide my face, but I would just have to accept that and keep going. I needed to get off this floor and out of this hospital.

"What are you doing?"

The voice was stern and demanding. I whipped around, terrified. There wasn't anyone there.

"Oh my gawd! Stop!" the voice demanded again, playfully. She wasn't talking to me.

Slinking back into the shadows, I found another way around the floor to a set of stairs, constantly on the lookout, and descended to the parking garage. Thankfully, I didn't have to exit through the front entrance. That would be difficult to explain to anyone who spotted me.

The garage was dark. The wind picked up as night encroached and fog poured over the ledges, manifesting along the ground. Taking advantage of the obscurity, I kept low. My bandaged legs didn't bend well, and the pain seared, but I kept moving. I needed to get away. My cellphone rang in the bag as I moved from the cover of one vehicle to another. Fumbling with the gauze, I grabbed the phone and saw the number. It was the same one that's been calling me for days. Unknown Caller from San Francisco.

Who the fuck are you?

My hands shook as my fingers closed in on the phone to answer.

"There you are!" a voice shouted. "What in God's name are you doing?"

I dropped the phone. The screen cracked and it slid under a car. I turned to see a woman in a white coat coming through the garage. I sunk as low as possible and scrambled out of sight. She continued her conversation passing me by, saying something about the noise and asking whomever to turn it off.

I curled against the concrete wall. I pulled my legs as close as possible and rocked myself back and forth. This was too much to deal with. I couldn't make heads or tails of anything anymore. My body was on fire and cold at the same time. It felt like the world was out to get me. I was vulnerable and alone, being stalked like prey by strangers and entities alike. I was feeling lost without

Collin. Taking a moment to breathe, I tried to pull myself back up after grabbing my phone.

It all happened so quickly, though. I'm not even sure where she came from. Her hands grabbed my neck and I felt my skull crack as my head was slammed into the car door.

"Caught you bitch!" Nadihne yelled.

***

I had worked with many models over the years, but Nadihne was different. She was always at the meet and greets, she networked like crazy, got invited to all the parties and accepted feedback graciously. Not to say that other models didn't, but it was different with her. Especially since she had spent months hanging out with me, Diego, and others to learn about our industry. She kept pace with every conversation she entered, understanding the lingo. Quickly, Nadihne was revered as a favorite amongst bay area local professionals, but there was something that still got under my skin with her. It was the way she looked at me whenever I was close to Diego. Was she jealous?

One night, I worked for a non-profit called DIFFA – the Design Industry Foundation Fighting AIDS. She had walked for one of the designers. As models left the runway, they came out in a specialized area, got their photographs taken while patrons mingled about and then headed backstage to change into their next looks. It was chaotic, but fun. I thrived on it.

As Nadihne came through, she stopped on her mark in a long, flowing lavender gown. Looking at me intently, I picked up the camera. In a sudden move, she grabbed the gown and flipped it into the air, giving it a dynamic shape. We did this dance for several minutes and she walked away without a word.

After the show concluded, I approached her. "You're really coming into your own with modelling."

"Thanks." She smiled. "I've been able to get a lot of work, and honestly, it's because of you."

"What do you mean?"

"You taught me things no one else would. All any other photographer has wanted was for me to pose and look pretty."

I nodded, grabbing a handful of hors d'oeuvres and began snacking. "Yeah, a lot of people can be like that. Don't let it get to you, though. They're doing their job."

"You're right." She muttered. "But they're so vicious and cutthroat about it all."

"Tell me about it." I rolled my eyes and laughed. "Look. Diego is having a party tonight at his place. A lot of people will be there. Feel free to swing by. You can make some new industry contacts and see if that doesn't open some more doors for you."

"You'd do that for me?"

I shrugged. "Honestly, it's not that big a deal. I hate going to these things and having someone there I can talk to will probably make my life a little bit easier."

That night, the music shook the walls of the apartment. Lights danced across faces and surfaces alike, and the temperature grew warm despite the cool air pouring in from the windows. I stood in the kitchen talking to Alonzo and Rina, but my eyes were glued to Diego. He was on the couch talking with a group of his friends. Sitting next to him was Nadihne, and his hand was placed gently on her knee. She sat confidently beside him as if she was always meant to be there.

My face grew hot with anger, and it drowned out the conversation I was having. Not trying to be rude, I excused myself and went to join Diego. I wrapped my arms around his back and sat on his lap as I laid a gentle kiss on his soft lips and smiled. He smiled back as I looked over his shoulder at a woman staring vehemently at me. If looks could kill.

I was right. She is after him.

"What's going on here?" I inquired playfully.

"We were just talking a little bit of business, but were getting ready to elevate this party a bit," he admitted.

"Oh? How so?" I teased.

A slender, sweaty man in a black suit smiled and pulled out a small bag of white powder. He asked if there were any takers. Diego laughed and agreed. So did Nadihne. I couldn't let her weasel her way into his life. Nervousness took over me. I've never done this before. I didn't want to.

"I don't know," I said apprehensively. "I'm not sure that's the right move for me."

"Oh c'mon," Diego chided. "Live a little."

Alonzo and Rina moved closer, watching studiously as I steeled my resolve. "Fuck it."

Grabbing a straw I leaned down against the tray and inhaled the first white line. Immediately, I regretted it. There was a burning in my throat and an almost instantaneous drip. My awareness was heightened and I took the second. A poisonous taste filled my mouth, my eyes watered and there was an insane head rush, like getting pummeled by ocean waves. All my senses sent me spinning and noise was amplified in my skull. I was high as fuck and on top of the world. I loved it. I focused on Nadihne's and Diego's faces. Sniffling, I looked at her and ran my tongue across my teeth. "Your turn."

Diego laughed. "Easy tiger, we're just trying to have a little fun."

"Mhmm," I responded as I straddled his lap. "I can show you a little fun."

Before I realized what was going on, I was gyrating on top of him, and my clothes were coming off. No one stopped me. Diego leaned back and enjoyed the show. I don't remember if the flashes of light were because of the drugs, the dance lights or people taking pictures. All of them felt in synch with this pleasure that coursed through me. I didn't care what others saw. What mattered was that Diego was mine and I wasn't about to let some up and coming model wreck my home. I continued to dance for him. My eyes closed. The world drifted away and when I woke up, I was in bed with Diego, completely undressed. And so was Nadihne.

***

"You know, you should never leave a hospital against medical advice, Tara. Especially since you were not properly discharged from the ward."

She wheeled me back into the green, dimly lit corridors of now bemoaning individuals suffering from their burns. It resembled being taken into damnation.

"What do you want from me?"

"From you? You have it all wrong. I don't want anything from you. I just need to make you better," she stated with disdain.

"Someone who wants to make me better wouldn't slam my head against a car."

"Well," she paused as we entered the room I had been occupying. "I admit, that was a little rash of me. However, you fucking deserved it for what you did to me back then."

"I don't know what you're talking about."

"Oh! Like you couldn't have warned me about him!" She snapped.

"You made your choice. And he wasn't yours to have in the first place, bitch! You weaseled your way into my relationship and I let go because he was no good. You should have seen that for yourself."

The blonde nurse looked back and forth at us without uttering a word. With her assisting the doctor, I was put back into the bed and restrained. The nurse left quickly to avoid unnecessary confrontation while Nadihne worked to have my bandages changed. She paused, taking in the state of my flesh.

"What the hell?" she questioned. Reaching for my head , she started tearing away at the gauze, unraveling the wrap to see my face.

"How is that even possible?"

"I don't know what you're talking about." I sneered.

"Bullshit! No one can heal burn scars that quickly!"

"What are you even talking about?" I rebuked again. Looking down at my wounds, they were bright red, aggravated and exposed. How did she not see that?"

"How did you heal so quickly? Huh? How is your face not marred by burns anymore?" she yelled and the questioning changed. "How is it that you were more liked in the industry that I was? I did everything right! I am prettier! I was nicer! I almost had Diego too! We could have lived a happy life together but you ruined everything! You ruin everything!" An unearthly gravel sprang into her voice as her shouts became more vehement. Nadihne was losing grip with her sanity. She jumped on the bed and started to choke me.

Her fingers dug into the soft flesh of my neck that was already open.

The pain was unbearable and blood poured out. I couldn't scream. My eyes rolled back as I started to black out. A hissing sounded again, this time, it became more garbled and distant, like something was blocking the noise.

Nadihne's face showed demonic pleasure. She smiled maniacally. Then she fell, slumping to the side. Megan was there, wide eyed and terrified, holding a bloody fire extinguisher.

CHAPTER 9

The metal canister echoed against the tile floor. Megan panicked and ran toward the hallway, shouting. "Sorry! I dropped something. Don't worry, I got it."

Returning to my side, she undid the restraints and started to whisper. "I leave you alone for one second! What the hell is happening here?"

"I don't know." Tears continued to stream down my face. At this point, it felt nonstop. "She's not a real doctor! She's someone I used to know. And now she thinks that I have super healing powers and went psychotic!"

"What?" Megan questioned. "That's…absurd…" Her words faltered as she looked closely. "Tara, your face."

I made my way to the bathroom again with Megan's assistance looking in the mirror. I saw a grotesque figure. Megan said I looked fine - just pinker than usual. Why were we seeing two different things? Was she gaslighting me?

Shaking my head, "No. I don't see it and right now, I need to get out of here."

The look on her face saddened. Megan wasn't trying to gaslight me. She saw what I couldn't see, but why?

"We'll figure it out together." Megan threw the plastic bag with my belongings on the bed and helped me get changed. She removed the bandages from around my arms and legs asking that I trust her. I was reluctant, but I agreed, and did my best not to look at the burns.

"Can you walk?" she asked.

"Yeah, just not well."

"Okay. Do your best to fake it till we get off this floor. I'll help the rest of the way."

"Thank you," I whispered as we moved in the dimly lit corridor where residents of the ward should sleep. Sounds of agony arose from every room we walked by.

Megan tensed, "This is frightening."

"Tell me about it."

The elevator at the far end of the hall chimed and a red triangle pointing down illuminated. We looked at it for a moment before the doors started opening.

"Pfft, that's not ominous at all," I snarked.

"This way," Megan stated as she guided me off the main hall. Shuffling down a side one allowed us to head toward the stairs. The glow of the exit sign never made me happier as we pressed the bar entering the illuminated stairwell.

Pausing, I breathed a couple of shaky breaths. Megan held onto my waist and held my hand that was draped over her shoulder. "How are you doing?"

I cried. "I want to go home."

"Me too," she replied with conviction. "We need to get out of here first."

The stairs were easier to use the second time around, but my body was still stiff and wouldn't bend due to the burns. I did my best to use the railing and hopped as fast as I could so that Megan didn't need to bear my weight any longer than necessary. Seven flights of stairs to the bottom and we were back in the parking garage where we dashed and hobbled to her car. Once inside, she didn't hesitate to get out of there and before long, we were back on the ferry and headed across the Puget Sound. The entire trip was done in silence. Making landfall back on Bainbridge Island, we went to her place where Laika was there, barking.

"She really is a good guard dog," Megan complimented.

"She's very protective of those she cares about." I smiled.

We settled in for the remainder of night. The next morning, she made sure I had clean clothes and fresh coffee. I used her bathroom and looked in the mirror. How did no one stop us coming out of that place, or on the ferry with me looking like this? I was afraid to take a shower - that the running water would agitate my scars and sores, so I used a damp cloth to gently dab myself. It stung, but not nearly as bad as I was expecting it to.

Megan sat, hunched over her tea, eyes transfixed into the distance as she stared into space when I joined her in the kitchen.

"Are you okay?"

She snapped upright out of her reverie clutching her chest. "Jeez, you scared me."

"Sorry," I replied, pouring a mug of hot coffee.

"It's alright. I was thinking about last night."

"Yeah? About knocking out the fake doctor?"

"That too," Megan said before sipping her drink. "But more than that. I'm not sure I understand what's going on here. Between the fake doctor, Collin, the day you nearly died from that gas leak or whatever-" She paused trying to wrap her mind around it. "I don't know. I think the answer lies back there in that house."

"No," I cut her off. "No freaking way."

"Let's grab Robbie and Kiera. Safety in numbers, right?"

"I'd rather call the cops! And you know as well as I do, that I can't do that. I'm supposed to be in a burn ward and you most likely killed someone last night."

"God, I hope not." She sipped her tea. "There was a lot of blood though."

Megan's eyes grew distant as she went back to looking inward and outward at nothing. Her face twisted as she contemplated the unfathomable situation that she found herself in. "Then Kiera and Robbie are our safest option. We'll take Laika with us too. She'll most likely sound the alarm if something is off, but we need to get to the bottom of this."

Grabbing my hand and holding it, unashamed of the scars and blisters, she smiled with those large teeth of hers and I couldn't help but crack a laugh. Megan was doing everything possible to keep me calm despite the storm that raged within her, wrapping her in anxiety and fear. I could see it written all over her face, and so, I conceded.

"Alright, let's go get them."

Laika waited patiently as her leash was latched onto her collar. Megan held it, because my hands wouldn't be able to grip it properly. "I'm not sure what it is that you are seeing Tara, but it's clearly not what I see."

"And that's the problem, Meg. I'm not sure which one of us is seeing what's real."

Robbie blared music in his garage, working on his bike. He moved and grooved as he torqued a wrench and focused on installing something new, I was just unsure of what. He turned, following the music and dropped his tool with a loud clank. "Holy shit!"

"Guess I'm not the crazy one today," I muttered to her.

"What the hell happened to you, Tara? You need a doctor!"

Kiera heard the racket and came to investigate. "Hon, is everything–Oh my god!"

"Looks worse than it feels," I tried to joke.

"We need to get you to a hospital," Kiera panicked as she turned to go grab a set of keys.

"Please, don't," I begged.

"We tried that," Megan stated. "The doctor literally tried to strangle her last night."

The couple paused, utterly perplexed.

"Look, I can cover myself again, if that makes it easier for you guys," I sighed. Reaching into my pocket, I pulled out the rolled up bandages from last night I kept on me and started to cover my face and arms. I continued to speak as I did, they watched in stunned horror. "What's really interesting is that I'm sure you two can see the burns and scars. Megan, cannot."

Their gaze darted to her. I could see their minds trying to figure out the disconnect.

"That's why we're here. I won't ask to come in, because I know how unsightly I am, but we need your help. Can we please have a few minutes of your time?" I asked.

Kiera surprised me by speaking first. "I don't know what you think we can help you with, but yeah. Come inside, let's hear what you have to say."

They did what they could to make us comfortable. Kiera found some fresh bandages in a first aid kit she kept and gave them to me to rewrap my wounds with, since the old ones were caked in dried blood. As I undid the dressing and re-mummified myself, I explained what happened over the last few days. Robbie remembered where the conversation started. He confirmed with me that there was no gas leak in the house.

As we continued, I shared the weird happenings with the design of the house and the artwork that showed up unexpectedly. Kiera was interested in the paranormal aspect of it.

"This sounds like the work of Onryō," she said delightfully.

"I'm not sure I share your enthusiasm, Kiera," I rebutted. "I'll get back to that but let me finish what I need to say."

Continuing, I covered the lost time, the nightmares, weird voices and sounds, feeling like I was constantly watched. I covered Collin's untimely demise and my time in the hospital last night. It was a lot to take in, and I felt crazy for saying it out loud.

The room went still; Kiera reevaluated her position on the Japanese ghosts. We all went quiet as we grieved Collin. The air was heavy, and then Robbie broke the tension. "What exactly do you want our help with?"

Megan responded. "I thought it over earlier. The house is the origin point for everything peculiar. We should go and see what has been happening there. No one has stepped foot inside in a couple of days. So, if it weren't the house, it would still be red, right?"

I nodded.

"Otherwise," she continued. "We can look around, see what has and hasn't changed and try to come up with a plausible explanation."

Robbie and Kiera shared a look that communicated something only lovers understood. Without a word, they looked away and agreed to assist.

We stood at the front of the large glass house and were stopped before we could get too close. An ominous energy was permeating from within. Chills went down everyone's arms. Something sinister was there and we could all tell. Laika growled, baring her teeth, hackles raised.

Megan dropped the leash. Laika ran around the back, we followed. Her continued barking led us to where she stood on the pier, barking into the Sound.

I sighed. "What has gotten into her now?"

"Shall we?" Robbie redirected.

Turning, we joined him at the front door where I opened it and stepped through. Glass crunched under our shoes. The remains of that night were still visible. Wine and blood stained the floor. Old pizza boxes and empty bottles lay strewn about. Pillows were missing from the couch.

"Looks like how we left it," I muttered. "Except for one thing."

"What's that?" Megan asked.

Seriously? Look around you, Megan.

"Everything is black," I muttered.

I wasn't sure where I wanted to start, so I went to the place I remember being last—the art room. From down the hall I could see the cocoon I had made myself and stepped closer. In the corner of the room was an easel with a picture. I moved closer and sighed. It was a charcoal gray background with the corrections of a portrait on it. I looked at it for what felt like an eternity, the eyes boring straight into me with seduction. Then I felt the pit in my stomach open up and my legs shook. It was one I did years ago when I first started this project. It was Diego.

The speed at which I turned and backtracked was astounding, but it wasn't fast enough. As I returned to the front room, I heard two quick bangs and consecutive thumps from upstairs. My heart sank, my body went numb, chills undulating down my spine and nausea set in. Fear froze me where I stood. Who was that? Should I call out? What if it was Robbie? Did he bring a gun? The silence in the house terrified me.

Creeping slowly and low to the ground, I found cover hiding behind the kitchen island beside Megan with her knees to her chest, trying to make herself as small as possible.

Slow and thunderous steps echoed overhead. We squeezed each other's hands and stayed curled up, out of sight. The steps moved from room to room. I could tell where it was, and it seemed to have stopped in the bathroom.

They began again, moving across the second floor, stopping at the top of the stairs. A heavy sniffing sound flowed down the steps into the kitchen followed by an unholy roar.

What the hell?

We held each other tightly, waiting for this beast to come. It didn't. Everything had gone quiet. I didn't move. Megan and I shared a look of terror, and I shook my head. I didn't want her to peak from behind the island. She nodded and smiled at me, trying to tell me without words that everything would be okay, to trust her.

I grabbed her sternly and shook my head, eyes wide with hysteria. It was not going to be okay. I had this feeling that it wouldn't.

Steady footsteps came down the stairs. Each one menacing, in its methodical pacing. Sonorous in its echo. I could tell it was him. Steeling myself, I stood and grabbed a knife from the counter and held it behind my back as I moved away from the kitchen to give Megan the best possible chance of escape. I backed down a hallway, avoiding the stairs, and made my way to the rear of the house. I opened and closed the door, so he would come looking for me, and I doubled back toward the front and into my workroom.

"Come out, come out, wherever you are." A sing-song voice of a man pierced the silence of the house.

Laika ran around the perimeter outside, barking wildly. She was never like this. Something was amiss. She never came close, but she was furious. Hackles still raised, snarling, foaming at the mouth. This wasn't her typical demeanor.

"That fucking dog!" he shouted. "Shut the fuck up!"

Another couple of shots rang out. Glass shattered and Laika yelped. My eyes widened at the worst. I didn't think my stomach could drop any lower. Another round of cold sensations overtook me in that instant. Luckily, I saw that she wasn't badly hurt. She did get grazed though, and began to limp off into the distance, seeking refuge.

She stood up for me. She has been my companion throughout the years, even helping me get through tough times with Diego and Nadihne. I wasn't about to let this manipulative piece of shit try to kill my dog! Without another moment to contemplate my actions I came out of hiding.

I didn't run; I didn't scream. I took a deep breath to maintain my composure and grabbed his picture from off the easel, stuffing the knife into my pants, behind my back, as I came to join and confront him.

"Diego," I said calmly while trembling on the inside. "What are you doing here?"

He turned at the call of his name. A gun in one hand. The other was bloody and gnarled with long fingers, monstrous in form.

"What the hell?" I whispered.

Was that the same hand that passed me a towel in the dark?

Diego smiled at me. "It's good to see you again sweetheart. It's been a while."

"Not nearly long enough," I stated flatly. "And I'm not your sweetheart."

Diego smiled and shrugged. "You'll always be my sweetheart. You know that."

His gaze turned icy.

"You still haven't answered my question. What are you doing here?" I asked as I moved slowly around the room, keeping him to the opposite side of me.

"I got word that you were hiding up this way. Figured I'd come say hi and see how you were doing."

"With a gun? How welcoming," I snarked. "How did you even get in here?"

Diego looked down at the weapon in hand and then smiled at me, head cocked, glaring. He put the gun down on the coffee table in front of him and sat on my couch, surrounded by black pillows. My gaze was glued to him but watched carefully for Megan's movement in my periphery. She snuck out from behind the kitchen island and up the stairs.

What are you doing, idiot? Get out of the house!

Sitting across from him, we exchanged predatory glances.

"Look," he started. "I didn't come here to argue with you."

"No, it looks like you came to murder me."

"That's not true."

"What happened to my friends?"

"Ok, that was an accident. They caught me off guard."

"You should have never been in here in the first place. And again, you haven't answered a single one of my questions. So, let's start again."

He shook his head and laughed silently to himself. I could see the incredulity on his face, but I wasn't falling for it.

As a narcissist, he belonged to a unique group of individuals. Most people who've dealt with one may not have realized that they may have had one or multiple in their lives early on, simply because a lot of them are good at hiding in plain sight until it's too late. However, once you've entered a romantic relationship with one, all of that is out the window, and you finally see the monster that you've inexorably been chained to. If you're lucky enough to pay attention.

They'd bait you with words and actions of love and admiration. They make you feel like you are their whole world. You complete them. Flattery became a weapon. What it really is, is love bombing, and they only use it to catch their prey, and to keep them when they've tried to break free from their clutches.

Once they have you, love stops, and the criticism begins. Nothing you do would ever be good enough. You would never be good enough. Appearances become everything and if you didn't start behaving exactly as they wanted you to, you would pay.

Lucky for me, Diego wasn't physically abusive often. If he left too many marks, people would know it was him. He tried his best not to go that route. Instead, he criticized me or avoided me when I needed to talk. Sometimes we might try to make plans and then he'd disappear, never reaching out to me until after that time passed, and then act like nothing happened. But it wasn't uncommon for him to hurt me physically too.

When we moved in together, it was worse. I did nothing right. I found myself apologizing for the inanest things, even if I wasn't at fault, just to keep the peace. If I had something negative to say, I was overreacting or being dramatic. He would deflect any blame or accountability. And what was worse than all of that, he could never say the two words that would have helped us both — 'I'm sorry.'

Here I was face to face with my tormentor of years. My heart raced, blood pumped in my ears, hands trembling. I took a deep breath again and remembered what therapy had taught me. I couldn't use emotion to win against a narcissist; he would twist my words and manipulate them to use against me. Logic didn't work either, because he played the perpetual victim. The only thing I could do, was maintain a cool and calm demeanor, never letting emotions get the better of me, and try not to fall for his tactics. However, it would probably result in him losing his cool, and that's when things got dangerous.

"Are you going to answer my questions?" I asked pointedly.

"If that's what you want, sure."

"It's not. What I want is for you to disappear, but I don't expect I'll get that lucky today, so I'll take what I can get."

"So spicy," he mocked.

I sat poised and emotionless, keeping my ears tuned for the slightest sound from upstairs.

"What are you doing here, and how did you get into my house?" I asked again.

"I really did come to see you. It's been years. I got a phone call yesterday that said you were in a hospital up here. They gave me your address, so I booked it up the coastline."

"Fucking Nadihne," I spat. "That…" I paused, realizing what was happening. I was being triggered emotionally, playing right into his hands. I couldn't let that happen. Taking a deep breath, I started again. "How did you get into my house?"

"You have a bad habit when it comes to spare keys."

"We haven't spoken in some time, and I recall telling you that I did not want you in my life." The words were tonally flat, rooted in honesty and delivered matter-of-factly.

"Here I was, thinking you were just being dramatic again, like you always are." He leaned back into the sofa, arms stretched out over the back of it. I ignored his deliberately jabbing words.

Don't do it! It's a fucking setup!

I cleared my throat. "I've only ever spoken the truth of what I have observed. Are you telling me that I should not trust my own judgement?"

"No, I didn't say that. Trust what you believe is true. Just don't forget, that perception can be clouded by emotions."

He leaned forward. A grin spread across his thin lips.

I took the time to notice that Megan was slinking down the stairs. She saw me and shook her head before heading around to the back of the house. Hopefully she makes her exit now. I stayed seated and choked back on my anger, putting the posterboard on the coffee table, facing Diego and clearing my throat.

"Do you know what this is?"

"Abstract art." He glared at me.

"Try again." I said coldly. "You know the answer."

A low rumble filled the silence between us. Clouds began to form and the large open room darkened drastically as we conversed in our tense states.

"An interpretation of me," he grumbled.

"Did you put it here?"

"Why would I do that?"

"Not the question I asked."

"No," he said scathingly. "I fucking hate that picture."

"Do you know how it got here?"

"No clue. It was already there when I arrived."

My head tilted, contemplating his words. If that were true, that means that he's not behind everything that's been happening to me, and I wasn't going out of my mind. Also, he had time and scoped out my entire house.

I know that Diego absolutely hates the picture of him I took to become part of this project. It was when the two of us went on our first date in Little Italy. We ate at a restaurant that made everything on the menu with garlic, even the desserts. I snapped a photograph of him just as our main dishes arrived. He was looking at me, longingly. It felt so authentic at the time, and now I knew it was a rouse. And he knew that I knew. That's why he hated it. It was a reminder that I knew he was full of shit.

"Hm. Okay," I stated.

***

Robyn and I were sharing the bathroom mirror. I busied myself with applying eyeliner, and she was trying to get her wavy locks to plump up with volume as she brushed them over her shoulder.

"So, tell me about this guy?" she asked.

"Um," I paused, fiddling with the pencil for a minute. "Well, he's hot."

"I would hope that he has a little more substance than hot if you're seriously in here for over an hour getting ready."

I blushed.

"He's a graphic designer, like you. He has dark features that draw you in, like, in a seductive way. Almost like hypnosis."

"Oh my god." Her face showed repulsion. "He didn't hypnotize you into going on this date, did he? That would be freaking creepy," she said and turned my way. "Look at me," she continued, "blink twice if you're in danger."

"Knock it off," I laughed. "It's not like that. He's not like that, I'm sure of it." Completing my make-up routine.

Walking back to the bedroom, Robyn perched neatly on the edge of the bed as I pulled outfits from the closet for peer review. I got a mixture of facial contortions, head bobs and hand gestures as we continued the conversation.

"You two met, how, exactly?"

"At the MAX convention in L.A. We happened to bump into each other during one of the lectures and started talking. Turns out that he lives and works here for one of the bigger firms that I've been trying to get hired for my work. He said that we should meet when we were both back in town, grab a bite to eat and talk about it."

"So, this is a business meeting?"

"Not quite," I said spinning around with another outfit in hand for Robyn's disapproval. I was not disappointed. "We exchanged information and we've been talking for a few months now, so we feel comfortable with each other. He asked me on a date, so I said yes."

"Do you know where you're going?"

"He told me about this spot in Little Italy that was recommended to him."

"Ok, so definitely worth dressing up for," she stated.

After some time picking out the perfect outfit, which ended up being a green dress and camel knee-high boots. I started to work on my hair when Robyn chimed in.

"You should really think about dying your hair."

I paused. "What's wrong with my hair?"

She shrugged. "I don't know. It just seems, mousey."

"Mousey?"

"Yeah, mousey," she reiterated.

I laughed at the incredulity. "Thanks for the feedback."

She disappeared again, and I stared in the mirror contemplating her words. Mousey? Putting it aside, I finished getting ready and hopped on the BART to Little Italy.

Once there, I texted Diego where I was. We had about twenty minutes before our date, but I wanted to make sure I got there early in case there were any delays. Besides, it was always better safe than sorry.

I tapped the concrete beneath my feet with the heel of my boot. The sound soothed me despite being irritated. I stood on the corner for over half an hour, clutching my phone. Where the hell was he? I checked the screen again, still no text.

I was ready to give up and go home when he came running my way, shouting my name. He was out of breath but still looked put together. He smiled as he approached and doubled over slightly.

"Hey, I'm glad I caught you. I was waiting at the other end of the street and didn't check this one."

"Oh. Well, I texted you a couple of times. Did you get them?"

"Urban canyons," he explained away. "Phone doesn't get reception here due to all the high rises."

"Right," I replied absentmindedly. "Of course not."

"Are you still interested in grabbing some dinner? I was able to swing by the restaurant on the way to this end and push the reservation a half hour."

"Sure." I smiled.

Something inside me felt a little off. It was nice that he came running here, and he still wanted to keep the dinner date, but at no point did he apologize to me. Was I mistaken in that? Or did he just brush off the situation?

He held his arm out for me to grab onto as he smiled. "Shall we?"

I smiled back. "Let's have a good time."

"Yes," he chuckled as we strolled the street together.

At the restaurant, we enjoyed drinks and appetizers as he told me about how he got into graphic design and why it appealed to him so much. He wanted to be known for great work, but he didn't want to be seen as a pretentious artist who sold crap for millions of dollars, claiming it was art. He valued working with multi-media projects to create unique products.

As the main courses came out, I saw his eyes widened as the dishes were set on the table before us. I snapped his photograph to see the genuine look of concern. I couldn't help but laugh. I think garlic is delicious.

"What's wrong?" I asked as I scooped up some mashed potatoes.

He shook his head. "I feel like I was misled a little about this place, that's all."

"How so?"

"Well, I was told its one of the better Italian restaurants around town, so I thought I'd bring you here to impress you. I didn't know we were getting ready to set out and vanquish vampires after this."

I laughed. It may have been a bit of a bitter sentiment, but at least he was being honest with how he felt. I began to feel overcome with a feeling, one that made me drop my guard around him. I was at ease. Diego smiled.

"I'll take us somewhere nicer next time. I promise."

"It's alright." I smiled. "I like the food. Besides, I brought breath mints, just in case."

"I might need about twenty," he replied, rolling his eyes.

"I appreciate the effort you put into this, Diego. Thank you."

He nodded his head and began to eat his steak. "No problem."

***

I looked down momentarily and realized that my arms were still bandaged. I forgot about the one on my face. Yet, here he sat, staring at me, not acknowledging the obvious. I couldn't help but think it was intentional. The way he looked at me made me question myself. There was this thought that creeped into the back of my mind, it caused me to fidget and look away from him despite wanting to maintain eye contact. I was self-conscious again. My pulse quickened beneath my skin and my chest tightened as I fought off the hyperventilating terror that tugged at my soul. He was stoic in his positioning and I couldn't stand it. Closing my eyes, I stepped back from my feelings, recognizing them but not succumbing to them. I breathed deep and centered my mind, not on doubts and feelings, but my presence.

Should I bring up my appearance to him? If I did, would that be seen as begging for attention again? Was I just calling out that he never asked me how I was doing, or would he say that I was seeking validation again and to stop being so fucking needy?

I stood confidently. "What happened to your hand?"

Diego seemed to just notice the unique appendage he had acquired. Studying it, he said, "I'm not entirely sure. But it's pretty cool though."

"You seem awfully calm for someone who has been disfigured."

"Look who's talking."

"Well, it's time for you to leave. You are not welcome here, and I have things that need to get accomplished."

I walked towards the kitchen stridently. He grabbed my wrist and pulled it to stop me. I looked down slowly.

With a calm and stern voice, I commanded, "Let go of me."

"Just wait," he snapped impatiently.

I pulled my arm back, and he held tight.

"No. I said let go."

"Will you calm down!" he yelled as he stood.

"Let me go!" I screamed. Panicking, my mind blanked, the only thing that I remember was the word 'survive'. I pulled the knife from behind me and sliced at his arm.

Blood sprayed across the floor and he retracted his hand. Clutching it, his face twisted and grew dark with anger. Then he smiled.

"There's the Tara I know," he scowled.

***

"All I'm saying is that, berating the waitress and calling her a 'stupid fucking cunt' loud enough for the rest of the room to hear, simply because she brought you guac instead of queso, wasn't necessary."

The keys fell onto a side table with a loud jingle as I opened the door to the apartment and walked inside, kicking my shoes off as I entered. Diego had once again made a scene so absurd and uncalled for that I felt uncomfortable, paid for my drink and appetizer quickly and left the restaurant embarrassed.

"That is not what I said!" Diego fumed.

"Yes, it is. Word for word." I barked back, tired of having to continuously do this with him. "You said, 'It's not even that hard of an order to get right the first time. How is she going to get my actual meal correct if she thinks that guac and queso are the same? The stupid fucking cunt should just go work somewhere else if she doesn't know that much. It's ridiculous.'"

I threw in some hand gestures to articulate the irritation that I felt in the heat of the moment. Diego sneered at me. His eyes darkened with hostility, and he made a low growling noise in the back of his throat. Clearly, I had hit a nerve, and he didn't appreciate my mocking him.

"I'm aware that you didn't use any hand gestures, Diego. You were too busy downing your second margarita, which was actually your fifth drink of the night because you had three cocktails here before we ever left the apartment."

I sighed and leaned against the far wall, my arms crossed over my chest.

"Here we go again," he exclaimed. "I wasn't drunk! Okay?"

"I never said you were."

"But that's your go-to argument. You blame everything on my drinking."

"If the shoe fits! And for the record, I don't always blame your drinking. I just point out what is a correlating factor to your behavior. If you don't like it, then fucking change."

I pushed off the wall and stormed down the hall slamming the bedroom door shut loud enough to create an echo and screamed into a pillow to let out my frustration. This was the fourth date that we'd gone on in the last two months that ended in disaster. The rage I felt was insurmountable. The embarrassment of being subjected to that behavior in a public setting made my skin crawl. He never saw his actions as a problem; they were always justified in some way because of the actions of others. He refused any kind of accountability, and I was irate at the absurdity of it all.

I didn't even bother getting undressed. I just crawled under the covers and cried. It wasn't supposed to be like this. Diego wasn't like this in the beginning. He was sweet and kind. I'm still able see that sweetness, and kindness, but it wasn't the only thing that I saw. I saw a broken man who didn't understand that he was the reason he was broken. I saw a man that found it more meaningful to appear successful and in control than to show vulnerability and uncertainty. He wasn't kind unless there was something in it for him. I saw a man who exerted cruel control.

I can't stand him. I can't stand being in this relationship. Why don't I just leave?

The rest of the evening was quiet. I fell asleep and woke up to find myself still alone in the dead of night. I could hear the television on in the other room. The cold hardwood floors and cool brass knob sent shivers through me as I opened the door. The sound grew louder and I peered down the hall. The blue light cast moving shadows on the wall, but Diego wasn't moving. I could see the toes of his shoes, then his ankles, knees, then his body slumped over. He was asleep on the couch. No, not really asleep, but passed out. It was different. He was sitting up, a half finished drink next to him. His head was forward, chin to his chest, snoring. That couldn't have been comfortable.

I saw the Diego I knew there, at that moment. The one who treated me kindly. The one who was nice, who told me he loved me with all his heart. I saw the man who needed me. The one who wanted me. I saw someone I wanted. He was someone who needed help.

"D?" I called meekly, pausing for a response. "D?"

He snorted in his sleep as he inhaled, a muffled moan escaped his lips, puffing them outward as he exhaled long and steadily.

"You need to come to bed," I said softly.

Another muffled response, halfway between the conscious and unconscious. Diego tried to stand but couldn't. I moved closer and helped him to his feet, wrapping his arms around my neck as I stood him up. My head tilted backward to keep his hands from slipping off.

As his eyes flitted open momentarily, he mumbled about work and those stupid bitches always being in his way. The smell of tequila and vodka kept assaulting my senses. My head reflexively pulled back and away to avoid another wave of the fumes. I gasped in abhorrent disgust.

"Yeah. We'll deal with them in the morning, okay? Right now, let's get you to bed."

"Fuck you, Tara." His words were slurred, but they still cut deep. "I don't need you to coddle me. You're just as bad as the rest of those fucking cunts. You're always looking down on me."

With a sigh, I replied. "No, I'm not. I'm only trying to look out for you."

It was quick. There wasn't time to process what happened until afterward. I was stunned, and it took a moment longer before I realized how much danger I was actually in.

His eyes held mine with a fury that I hadn't seen before. His pupils had expanded in a terrifying way, making his eyes nearly pitch black, reminiscent of a shark. I was frozen like a deer on a dark road met with headlights. His hand wrapped around my throat, squeezing my vocal cords, rendering me silent. My feet came off the ground, and I felt the sharp stab of electronic and glass shards in my head and neck. I crumpled to the floor amidst the wreckage of the television and porcelain, gasping for air, cutting myself more as I tried to get away.

My neck hurt when he grabbed my hair and pulled me down the hall. I screamed, kicked, and clawed to be let go. He didn't. Instead, he somehow found the strength to throw me on the bed. Climbing on top of me, his necrotic exhalations making my eyes water and throat gag, he blocked my ability to get away. His lips pressed against mine fervently. I could feel him trying to get inside me. First the boney and intrusive machinations of his hand. I fought back, mustering what strength I had to push him off of me, trying to get away, screaming inside and crying out for him to stop. He grabbed my arms and pinned them down before forcing himself further on me, violating and invading me.

Laika growled and jumped on the bed, biting Diego in the calf and pulling, forcing him to be distracted momentarily, but not long enough. He screamed out and kicked Laika in the head. She whimpered and fell sideways, unmoving.

"Laika!" I screamed.

Diego didn't miss a beat and continued.

He let out a satisfied moan. As his head lowered toward mine. Anger consumed me, a fire fueled me. In that brief second I bit his ear and pulled with all my might. This was my opportunity and I wasn't going to waste it. He yowled and released my arms. I slapped him so hard that it echoed. His head turned sideways and he paused, fumbling backward, the monster inside Diego backed away.

I clawed at the covers, pulling them close to my chest for security, folding my body tightly into a ball, eyes red and unblinking as I stared at him with pure unadulterated hatred.

"Fuck you," he mumbled after me before shutting the door and stumbling back down the hallway, disappearing into the dark.

Every part of me collapsed and broke down. The physical pain was nothing. My body had numbed it all as a survival mechanism. The only pains I felt were the excruciating, gut punch of betrayal, the adrenal kick from my fight or flight mode releasing chemicals in a mass flush and the destruction of the security I felt in my own skin. I was violated.

I crawled across the floor to Laika and held her in my arms. Sobbing, I pet her as she looked at me. She wasn't hurt too badly, only stunned. Those big, brown soulful eyes looked at me, conveying a sorrow and worry that I couldn't fathom.

"You're a good girl," I cried into her fur. "Thank you."

I stroked her soothingly. She thumped her tail once, softly.

Was this how my efforts to help would always be rewarded? What did I do that was so wrong this time to deserve this? Why me?

The next day, I showed up to work in a turtleneck, covering the marks on my body to the best of my ability. I was sleep deprived and disheveled, but I didn't care. I made a vow to myself not to let him have control over me ever again.

I set my bag down in the cubicle and sensed a lot of gazes on me. I looked up to see groups of people talking to one another who quickly turned away. Even Alonzo and Rina kept their distance. One person moved closer.

"Hey, Tara," he called.

I tried to recall his name, but it was difficult in the moment The pudgy build and thinning hair, wire frame glasses, it had to be Mike. He wasn't someone that I interacted with often, but he did have a management position, so I should probably be courteous, just in case.

"Good morning," I sniffled. "How can I help you, Mike?"

"Well, that's what I came to ask you. Diego spoke with us about what happened between the two of you last night…"

I raised a hand to stop him from speaking any further.

"Diego spoke with you?" I asked for clarification. A tone of irritation and incredulity in my voice.

"Yes. He spoke to the entire management team."

"Okay," I sighed as I sat, my mind racing with possibilities of the lies he spun. Every narcissist plays the victim, so this should come as no surprise to me. "And what did he say?"

Mike cleared his throat and sat on the edge of my desk. I looked at his butt resting there and then stared at him. He stood without a word. "He told us about how you berated him and were emotionally abusive; that you physically assaulted him last night. Diego has a pretty good bruise on his face from where he says you slapped him, and then there's the teeth marks on his ear."

"He's lucky that's all that happened to him," I scowled.

"Excuse me?" Mike was caught off guard. I'm pretty sure he wasn't expecting me to admit I did anything or that I'd say it wasn't me.

"I'd do it again, too!" I shouted. "You want to see abuse? Here! Let me show you!" I pulled down the sweater to showcase the handprint imbedded in green and purple on my neck. "Or how about the scabs on the back of my head from when he threw me into the fucking TV? Or maybe these?"

Anger boiled inside me as I showed off the marks and scars, pulling up the sweater sleeves to display the matching bruises on my wrists. "I'd love to show you the marks between my thighs right now, but I don't want you to think I've sexually assaulting you too, Mike. I didn't abuse him. I fought back!"

The manager took a deep breath and stepped back, clearing his throat. "I understand that this is a very emotional time for you. I am not here to take sides."

"But you already did!" I confronted him. "Didn't you? You believed him because he was here first to tell his sob story. You can't even bring yourself to look at me right now."

Mike kept his eyes lowered, unable to look at the marks, bruises, or the anger and sadness on my face. That's all the proof I needed.

"Yeah, well, that's okay. Fuck you guys too! I quit!"

Grabbing my bag, I stood and stormed out. Whispers trailed behind me, calling me crazy and saying that I was losing it. I continued shouting about the unfair treatment of women and how they didn't even bother to try and get my side of the story. It probably didn't help me look less like a crazy perpetrator in the moment, but I was furious.

Back at his apartment I packed all my things. I put them in my car and left the key behind. Laika sat in the passenger seat trying to lick the tears off my cheeks as I drove. I didn't bother trying to stop her.

A short while later, I pulled up to a house in Twin Peaks and Robyn rushed out to meet me. Without a word, she put her arms around me and held me as I fell apart.

***

He lunged for the gun on the coffee table, I stabbed the knife into his shoulder blade, forcing him to falter. He cried out again and I stole the gun.

Running outside of and around the back of the house, I saw that Megan had disappeared. So did Laika. Luckily, Megan left me a note scribbled in the sand, 'called 911'. I breathed a sigh of relief, help should arrive shortly. All I had to do was stay out of the house and keep distance between the two of us.

Tossing the gun into the water, I felt a push from behind. I crawled to escape, but I was overpowered. My mind raced with all the previous fights I had with him that got physical and the panic took my ability to breath away. Diego had a hold of me and started dragging me deeper into the freezing wake. It shocked and incinerated every nerve ending in my body. I cried in agony as the salt water seeped into my wounds.

"You've always had a problem with overreacting. And now, look what you've made me do!" He yelled.

My head was shoved under the waves as I thrashed about beneath him, screaming into the murk. Something heavy pressed against my back. Was that his knee? No. It was heavier than that, and then it rolled off.

My fingers clawed through the rough sand and thick clay, grappling tightly at the malleable mud as I broke free from the surf and gasped for air. The fire in my chest extinguished with that first deep inhalation. Megan stood there. She was always there for me. Slowly she tried to back away. Diego rose again, fuming with rage. He turned to her.

"You shouldn't have done that," he snarled animalistically.

With all the strength he could muster, he swung his arm and hit her in the face. The force of the impact sent her falling backward. I jumped on top of Diego, enraged, screaming and pounding against him. I pulled the knife from his shoulder and punctured his back again, and again.

He faltered forward and stopped moving. I retrieved the knife.

"Megan!" I called, scrambling to her side. "Are you alright?"

She had a good-sized bruise on her neck and face, with some scratches, but she seemed to be okay. Looking up, she focused and her eyes went wide, pushing me away.

One, two, three, four, five shots rang out. Then the gun faltered.

"Fuck!" Diego screamed.

I watched with sheer horror as Megan lay lifeless on the ground, red ichor spilling and staining the beach. Unable to control myself, I wailed again, delirious. Diego used the opportunity to trap me beneath him, hitting me repeatedly in the face with the gun.

My head spun as blood seeped from my bandages again. He pulled his arm upwards and back to swing again. His face contorted with rage as his lips parted to spew his hatred at me.

"You've always been like this…" he stopped.

***

Our shoes were soaking wet, and I could feel the water seeping through my socks as we ran across Ghirardelli Square. We laughed and sought refuge from the sudden storm inside the chocolate shop. While there, we each ordered a hot fudge sundae and spoke.

Today, Diego and I were supposed to check out the Museum of Modern Art, hit Ghirardelli Square, Pier 39 and Fisherman's Wharf, then hop a ferry over to Sausalito for some wine tasting and shopping. However, with the weather making such a drastic change, who knows what we'd be able to go do anymore. He saw thoughts racing through my mind and placed a hand gently on top of mine.

"Hey, you alright?"

I snapped out of my train of thought and looked at him smiling. "Oh yeah, I'm fine. I was just thinking about what to do now that it's raining."

"Rain doesn't have to stop us from enjoying our day, you know? If it wasn't for the rain, we probably wouldn't be enjoying these sundaes right now, would we?" He smiled.

"Yeah, you're probably right about that."

"Thank you." Diego grinned triumphantly at the acknowledgement. "Was there something special that you wanted to do today that you have a concern about doing now, because of the rain?"

I paused for a moment contemplating the agenda that the two of us sat down and made together over the phone a week ago. "I think going on a ferry ride isn't the brightest idea. The bay gets pretty choppy on a normal day. With a storm, it might be worse."

He pondered my response while he took a spoonful of vanilla and fudge, savoring it together. "Okay, so the boat ride is out of the question."

"There's nothing that should stop us from enjoying the pier though. We just need to wait out the rain," I contemplated.

"Good luck with that," a stranger who overheard our conversation said. "Newest weather update says it's not supposed to let up until after nine tonight."

"Damn," Diego muttered.

"Yeah," I admitted defeatedly.

Our sundaes began to melt into a congealed mess in the glasses. We both stirred them absentmindedly in the silence of our conversation. I glanced his way to see that he shared the same vacant expression I had. He was trying to decide on an alternative plan on the fly.

"I got it," he said confidently. "Let's finish our sundaes quickly and get out of here."

"And then what?" I asked with a spoon in my mouth.

"It's a surprise," he grinned.

The two of us headed back to his car. He didn't seem to mind that we were soaked through and through, and it might damage his seats. Turning the heat on, he pulled out of the parking spot and made his way south onto Highway 1.

It's one of the more scenic drives in California, because it runs right along the coastline. There are times where it veers a little more inland and you have to watch for rock slides, but the drive is beautiful. We made our way down past Davenport, Half Moon Bay, Santa Cruz and Big Sur – some of the more iconic stopping points in Northern California along the coast. We drove for about two hours. I lay back and rested, letting the heat dry my clothes as I listened to the rhythmic rain fall on the windows and drifted in and out of rest.

Diego woke me. I opened my eyes to see that we were parked at the Monterey Bay Aquarium. I told him once before that it was one of my favorite places to visit when I had free time, because it brought me a sense of calm to witness the life of underwater animals.

"If we can't go on top of the waves, we might as well go under them. Right?" Diego looked at me and smiled, his teeth gleaming, his eyes gentle. He really listened to me.

I smiled and gave him a kiss. "You didn't have to drive us all the way down here Diego!"

"I know I didn't. But I wanted to."

We got out of the car and went inside. We spent a long time in front of the exhibits, just watching the motions of creatures as they flitted effortlessly through the water. At the center of the aquarium was a set of steps and we sat on them for over an hour, talking. In front of us was a large tank for viewing, but it wasn't actually a tank. It was an enclosure of the natural bay. It had large growths of seaweed and kelp, animals that were local to the region, rock formations and sharks that would come and go. Occasionally, divers would enter, wave to the crowds and we'd wave back as the divers either worked on marine biology projects, or diving certification requirements. It was always fun to sit and watch.

We sat there speaking to each other at length, watching the world go by, smiling, and laughing. When I finally got sore from sitting, he let me lead the way to the next exhibits. We saw jellyfish, sharks, deep sea exhibits, the aquatic petting zoo and many others before we made our way topside to the same enclosure we sat in front of a while ago. A crowd had gathered. We moved closer out of curiosity.

We got to see it, there in the enclosure. It was a once in a lifetime experience. The waves of the bay crashed against the rocks, but the aquariums bay enclosure allowed for refuge from the harsher elements. The surface was smoother, but still rocked a bit. The rocks that separated the aquarium from the rest of the Pacific Ocean made a nice respite for a wild sea otter who found her way into the calmer space to give birth.

This was a spectacular moment to be a part of, because normally, wild animals don't give birth in places where others can see, but we watched the whole thing unfold in front of us, in the rain on the coast line, witnessing the miracle of life.

"This is amazing," I said with admiration in my eyes.

Diego wasn't looking at the otter, but instead at me. "You're amazing."

My head swiveled, unsure of whether or not what I heard was what he said. A quizzical look on my face, must have given him all the context he needed, so he laughed lightly and repeated himself.

"You are, Tara. You're amazing, and I'm in love with you."

I stood a little taller as the words seeped into the deepest recesses of my mind and shot warmth through every fiber of my body. I blushed. I could feel it. My lips curled upwards as I hugged him, planted a kiss on his neck and whispered in his ear. "I love you too."

***

Diego looked down, startled and shocked to see the knife I drove into his chest. His eyes fixed on mine. Pulling the knife out,

I stabbed him again. I could see that he wasn't going to make any other moves, and then I twisted it in his heart. Finalizing his death.

"Fuck you!" I managed to call out.

My ex went still and collapsed sideways with a thump. His weight was heavy to remove from on top of my legs. I lay there momentarily, trying to wrap my head around everything that happened, unable to truly grasp it.

Rain fell. I flinched having forgotten about the rumbles I heard earlier. I was going to need to get to shelter, or I might start hurting more than I already was. The salt water in my exposed wounds hurt, but having rain fall in tiny little piercing droplets against my skin and gauze would be torture.

Fire coursed through me. Every muscle strained and shook as I mustered the strength to get to my feet. Deep lines were carved in the sand from our scuffle and where I drug myself. Blood trailed into the surf from all three of us. Pulling myself up to Megan's body, I apologized and wept. Why did she have to save me?

"I'll be back for you, I promise."

It hurt, but I slowly got to my knees and forced my body to a standing position. Keeping my eyes fixed forward, I moved towards the house. That's when I heard a groan I wasn't expecting. Was she okay? How did she survive that?

Turning, I saw the unexpected.

Diego's body began to rise from the sand, clutching at his chest. Thunder rumbled louder this time, nearly on top of us. The sky went pitch black and a bolt of lightning pierced the sky.

As the flash dimmed, I could see that I wasn't looking at Diego anymore. I was looking at me dressed in a sagging purple sweater, ripped jeans, mousy brown hair in a wet pony tail and the same hazel eyes. I took the knife from my chest and tossed it aside. We locked gazes–mine with absolute fear, hers with contempt.

"That fucking hurt."

CHAPTER 10

There were no words to describe the sheer terror and confusion I felt. There were no smoke and mirror tricks, no hallucinations – I think, and no getting away. After this entire week of nightmarish events, I was now forced to confront myself.

Scrambling backward, the rain still pelting me, I looked into the eyes of my doppelganger and screamed. She stopped moving forward. Crossing her arms, she looked at me with annoyance and huffed. An aura of dismissiveness radiated off of her.

Is that how I look when I get irritated?

"Calm down," she said sternly. I said? We said?

I scuttled further back, turning over as I rushed to my feet. The house was going to be my safest place despite knowing that it wasn't safe at all. If I got back around front, the police should be pulling up at any moment. I could wave them down. There was no time to hesitate, I needed to find a way out of this situation.

Hobbling across the yard, I ran past the window that Diego shot, but it wasn't broken anymore. There was no glass in the yard. I ran further up the drive to get away from that haunted abode and wait for the police while hiding among the tree line.

I cowered behind some bushes and I waited, trying not to go mad as my brain spiraled. I waited there for what felt like ages.

No flashing lights, no sirens, no tires on pavement seemed to come. Then I listened more intently.

Not only were there no expectant sounds of assistance, but there was also no sound of trees rustling. The waves of Elliott Bay were silenced. There were no birds or insects making noise, no pattering of the rain on leaves, only darkened skies and silence. Slowly, I elongated myself from my hiding place to see what was going on.

I looked around and found myself in pitch darkness. The sky flashed occasionally with lightening, but there was no sun and no sound.

Am I deaf? Did getting knocked about damage my hearing?

I took a bandaged hand and clapped it gently against my ear. I could hear the thump of the pressure in my ear and knew it wasn't me. I sighed briefly and looked down the drive towards the house.

I must not have been paying enough attention because there I was, standing mere feet away from me, one leg cocked in front of the other, arms folded impatiently against my chest.

"Are you done, yet?"

I was caught off guard. Was this clone not concerned with whatever was going on around us? I watched her meticulously as she moved. She had the same gait I did, always stepping forward on her left foot first. I was stunned to be coming face to face with myself.

She sighed and stepped closer. I flinched. "Relax. I'm not here to hurt you like they did. Honestly, I can't do any worse than what I've already done."

Her head hung, momentarily, saddened by something. I didn't know what. She shook off the invisible weight she was dealing with and made eye contact. "Look, do you want answers or not?"

Silently, I pondered as she extended her hand to me.

"How do I know that I can trust you? How are you even real?"

"Trusting me is subjective at best. Honestly, everything is. But ask yourself this; does any of this feel or look real to you right now?" she fired back. "Tara, you can barely trust yourself, I know. That's why you are fighting me. However, if you want this all to end, you need to be willing to let go of control. That's kind of my thing."

I reluctantly gave my bloody and bandaged hand to her. She pulled me in closely in a quick jerking movement and hugged me. She didn't make any other moves. Her arms enveloped me, and I, her. Then she whispered into my ear gently, "I'm sorry."

I hurried to get away, thinking she was going to kill me, but she didn't. The other Tara stood there and let me go from her grasp, tears in her eyes.

"What do you mean, you're sorry?" I was choking on my words, a massive lump forming in my throat.

"C'mon. I'll show you," she insisted.

I followed her back to the house, apprehensive of everything. I kept looking around to see that the world had all but paused around me except for the lightning, and the two of us. She ushered me back into the house, where warm white light washed over us. She offered me something to drink, which was wild, because it's my fucking house!

The other Tara poured two glasses of red wine, and set them on the kitchen island. With fingers gently touching the stem, she glided one across to me.

I went to grab it, but she shouted, "Wait!"

Coming around and in front of me, she started to pull the bandages off. A part of me wanted to argue and fight about my grotesque appearance, but there was something about her, that was starting to calm me down and allowed her to remove them. I put a little trust in her not to hurt me.

After my head was unwrapped, she moved to my arms. As I watched, I saw that my arms were no longer marred with burn marks. Completely flabbergasted, I rushed to the bathroom just down the hall and looked into the mirror.

I was me again. The same mousey brown hair and hazel eye reflection I knew greeted me. I no longer had half a face that was disfigured and oozing. My skin was smooth like porcelain. But how?

Returning to the kitchen, the other Tara was finishing her glass of wine and pouring another. I came closer, slowly as I tried to understand the situation.

"You good?" she asked.

"I'm not sure. Should I be?"

I sat across from her and sipped my drink.

"That's a relative question, honestly. Let me ask you this first. Did the hissing in your ear ever stop?"

I sat up straight and locked my gaze on her. How could she know about that?

"Um, yeah?"

"Do you remember when?" she followed up.

"I think it was just a little bit ago. Everything went still. I couldn't hear anything."

"Shortly after I showed up?"

"Yeah."

"That figures," she replied solemnly.

"Who or what exactly are you?"

The other Tara only smiled and drank her wine. "To answer that question, we need to take a look at everything else that's happened this week. Are you ready for that?"

"Do I have a choice?"

She smirked. "Not really."

With a gentle nod and a gulp of my wine, my glass tapped against the counter. "Where do we begin then?"

"Right here," she said solemnly as she gestured around. "Take a look around and tell me what you see."

I scanned everything in the kitchen. I turned behind me and viewed the living area as well. Nothing escaped my scrutiny. I walked the halls, stiffly for a moment and then paused. I still had gauze wrapped around my legs. After removing those bandages to find smooth skin again, I laughed in disbelief.

"What the actual hell is going on?"

Out of the corner of my eye, the other me showed up and waited. She didn't say anything, only made her presence known. It was unmistakable.

"Everything is back to the way it was, but the color changed again."

"Anything else?" she asked.

My eyes widened. Robbie and Kiera! Diego shot them, and their bodies were still upstairs. I bolted up the steps skipping two at a time and ran from room to room. No one was there. There wasn't a single blood stain anywhere. I ran back down and out the back door of the house towards the shoreline. Where was Megan? Her body was gone. The sand was still red from where I bled, but that was it.

She followed me outside, and I could feel her presence behind me.

"This doesn't make any sense. Where are they?"

"Who, Tara? Be specific."

"My friends!" I shouted with confusion. "Where are my friends? Robbie and Kiera were upstairs when I heard Diego shoot them. And, and, Megan," I stammered. "Megan was right here! I watched her die!"

The sky brightened with another flash of lightning; it looked to light up the entire island. We mimicked one another as we shielded our eyes. As the flash faded, the other me looked up momentarily, saddened. "C'mon, we better hurry. There aren't going to be too many more of those."

"What?" I asked as I followed her back inside.

In the art room, she made herself comfortable at the computer. I paused at the entry when I saw the easels with the art work on them. Seven in total. Each one a different color. There were only six different figures though. They were all aligned for me to view. Tara cradled her head on her hands and watched me move closer.

I looked at each one carefully. It took me a second, but I noticed that the colors correlated to the colors that the house turned - indigo, orange, gold, red, black and violet. There was a green one there too, and I looked closer at it. It was the image I retouched of Nadihne years back. Was that a coincidence?

I turned to look at the other me. She busied herself on the computer, not making eye contact. I turned back to the images.

Something inside me tugged. A memory? A voice? It was both. A conversation that I had with Megan when I was still new here.

"I wanted to experiment with color and the feelings that each one evokes," I recalled.

The other me looked up. She didn't move, but she made eye contact, nodding to let me know that I was on to something. I went back to the images and paced. Back and forth, my gaze danced across the forms. There was something there, but I wasn't quite sure. What was it.

"Wait!" I paused. "I remember taking each one of these images."

"I would hope so. They're your work."

"Not what I meant," I quipped back. "Each one of these pictures has a special meaning to me. This one of Diego was from our first date and I had an inclination that he was no good, but ignored my gut feeling. This picture here of Nadihne led me to suspicions that she was up to something, before she tried to wreck my relationship. This one here…" I trailed off.

The ruby red background offset the stark black and white marks of a man who smiled handsomely at me. He was reclined and even in the photograph, his eyes shined with adoration. Tears fell freely at the memory of Collin and this image. We had such a wonderful day that day.

***

Collin came by to pick me up and surprised me with three different bouquets of flowers.

"I wasn't sure what kind of flowers you liked, so I got you several." He said sheepishly.

I laughed and smiled. "I love it. Thank you." Leaning forward I hugged him and kissed his cheek. His warmth enveloped me. His arm wrapped around me, holding me sturdy and close while his scent put me at ease. The skin of his face was rough but also smooth from recently shaving. His eyes looked around nervously and I held his gaze.

"Let's get these into some water and then we can go."

Turning back inside, I found an empty vase in the hall, grabbed it and a pair of sheers from the kitchen drawer. Usually, I used these for cutting meat, but this would have to do for now.

Collin washed the container for me and filled it with water and plant food. I angled the cuts on the stems and passed them over to him to carefully place in an arrangement. I was surprised to see three dozen flowers in one vase, but he made it work. I smiled and placed it on the coffee table so that I could see it every time I came downstairs and every time I came home.

"You're the best," I smiled at him.

"I try." He grinned back.

Letting out a deep huff of air, relieved that I liked the gift, he grabbed my arm and gave me a kiss on the lips. I melted into him.

Our bodies pressed closely together, and then it stopped. He looked at me, face flushing red and stammered through an apology. I calmly touched his chin and directed his attention back to me as I kissed him again.

That afternoon we spent hiking on a trail at Mt. Rainier with Laika. We found a beautiful glen to rest in and lay amongst the flowers. I started snapping photographs of Laika bounding through the foliage. Just as I turned my attention towards the horizon, a break in the clouds above let a single beam of light down across Collin in the field. It was nearly cinematic in its portrayal. Gray clouds above, a blue-green background and a handsome man splayed out before me in a golden ray. I snapped many images.

Collin just smiled and let me do my thing. When I was done and happy with what I got, I sat next to him, packing up my gear.

"Did you get a good shot?" he asked.

"I think so."

"Okay. I can't wait to see the end product. That's what you call it, right?"

I chuckled. "Yeah, it is."

"Cool."

He pulled me back down. My head resting on his chest, his heart beating in my ear, steady, but slightly quickened.

"Collin, are you okay?"

"Yeah, I'm fine. Why?"

"Your heart is beating a little fast, is all."

"Oh." He paused. "Well, that's probably just nerves." He flailed his hand in the air dismissively.

I caught his hand and started tracing his palm with my fingertips before lacing our fingers together and kissing his hand. "What are you nervous about?"

Laika came back, trotting close by and laying down next to us panting heavily. She was happy, there was no mistaking that.

"I wanted to ask you something, and um, I don't know, I'm just nervous."

"Okay? Why not take a deep breath, count to three and just blurt it out?" I mentioned.

"Just blurt it out?" He chuckled nervously.

"Yeah. Sometimes it's easier that way. It's sort of like ripping off a band-aid. There's less pain in the end that way."

"Yeah, sure," Collin sighed. Taking a deep breath, I could hear him whisper a count of three and then he blurted it out. "I think I'm in love with you and want to become your boyfriend to explore that together. To explore something more meaningful, together. But only if you are willing. I know you went through something rough, and trust may not be the easiest thing for you right now, but I want you to trust me and trust us."

I dropped his hand gently, unlacing our fingers and sat up. Turning, I could see the look in his eyes. There was terror of rejection. There was no going back from this. He said it, and it's out there now. I was shocked. I sat with the words for what felt like ages and I just looked at him before I gently straddled him and smiled.

"Yes."

"Yeah?" He smiled nervously.

I reassured him that my answer was a resounding yes. We kissed and hugged and rolled in the field until the sun set and had to make our way back down the paths.

***

"This image represents love," I muttered.

"It's more than that. Keep going," she barked at me.

I turned towards the easels again. I contemplated. It's more than people. It's more than emotions. Thinking through the process, I started at the far left. What was it? An indigo palette. The figure? Alonzo.

Where was the photograph taken? Why was it taken?

Moving over, the golden silhouette of Raina, smiling smugly.

"Oh yeah! I remember now!" I turned towards myself with the revelation. "These were taken at work! Alonzo was given extra work, but then threw a hissy fit because he wasn't going to get paid extra to compensate for the amount of work that was being asked of him. He got screwed once before and wasn't going to allow it to happen again. He set out to do the bare minimum after that. I can still hear the sassiness of his voice telling the managers off. Raina was there and she jumped at the opportunity because she was gunning for a promotion."

Laziness and greed.

Next to that was an image of me. A rare one that I never showed anyone, yet here it was. Inspired by the photographer Nan Goldin. I took a photograph of myself shirtless the day I moved back in with Robyn. I documented the abuse I received that had opened my eyes. However, there was a darker history to this picture. One I refused to admit to anyone else; that I tried to work things out with Diego. He promised he'd change, that he would do better by me, and I wanted to give him the benefit of the doubt. I was hopeful. I was naïve. I was a glutton for punishment because it wasn't the last time he hurt me, and I thought that that, was all I deserved in life.

Scanning the rest of the stands, I stopped.

"Tara?" I asked.

"Yeah?"

"Earlier you asked if anything felt real or not."

"Mhmm," she acknowledged while scrolling on the computer.

"You also said, that things were subjective, right?"

"I did."

A bright light filled the room. It flashed and flickered for longer than a typical lightning storm flash would. The other Tara looked outdoors, concerned before breathing a heavy sigh of regret.

"You also said, you couldn't hurt me any more than you already have, right?"

"Correct."

She turned and focused on me. Without missing a beat, she moved away from the computer and sat on the couch, motioning for me to join her.

"I think I'm starting to understand what you meant." My throat tightened as I uttered the words. I choked a little, forcing a cough to clear my airway.

"How long have I been dead?"

She shook her head solemnly sighing. "You're not dead, Tara."

"I'm not?"

"No. Not yet anyway, but soon."

"Well, how do I fix this then? How do I wake up? What do I need to do? Tell me!" I pleaded.

She only sat forlorn across from me. Brown strands of hair covered her eyes and she wept, her head shaking with resignation. "I'm so sorry."

"No," I begged. "No. Please! Don't do this to us!"

"I can't fix it," she cried. "I tried! I've manifested myself several times: in the coffee shop, at the tower, in your bathroom, beside your bed, and in what you thought were dreams. I tried to scare you awake, and I couldn't."

"That was you? All of that was you?" I muttered with confusion.

The anger and frustration I felt was insurmountable. My mind reeled. Another flash of light. The other Tara looked, she panicked.

"Tara, you need to stop!" I could feel the tension in her voice. Not only was it in her, but it resonated inside me. "If you keep this up, you'll run out of time much sooner!"

"I don't understand!" I cried. "Help me understand!"

"It's your stress! You are burning out faster than necessary!"

It broke me to watch my own visage tormented in a way that I inexorably understood. We shared the same body and mind. We were one. I finally knew who she was. She was Pride, and she was hurting too. I tried to give myself a hug and let her know that we were in this together.

I pulled her into an embrace. She sobbed into my shoulder, and something began to happen. She diminished in my grasp, fading, fusing with me back into one individual. I could hear her say one last time, "I'm so sorry."

I collapsed.

***

Everyone had cleared out from the photo shoot on Deception Pass. I passed off all the paperwork to the park ranger after having done the last walkthrough together to make sure there wasn't anything left behind or damaged. He was very courteous even though we went over on our allotted time by about a half hour. When he was satisfied and all my documents were signed clearing us from any potential damages, I headed back to my car.

As I was seated, I watched the fog form again.

"Shit! I'm going to have to hurry."

I grabbed my phone and sent a text to Collin. 'Shoot went great. I can't wait to get this campaign out there. I think you'll like it too. Will show you tonight. Can't wait to see you. Be home soon.'

I plopped my phone in the passenger seat on top of the folder of documents I needed to file in the studio tomorrow and started the car. The engine took a little longer than I liked warming up, but once it was ready, I pulled out of the parking spot and began my trek across the bridge.

Deception Pass is a bridge that is formed in two segments over the Puget Sound with a curve in it that goes over a large rock outcropping in the middle. It forces you to slow down or risk getting into an accident. Honestly it was a horrible design because coming in one direction, the turn is blind and you descend, coming in the other, you're forced uphill and can't see. Either way, it's treacherous. Having to do this in the fog was going to be trickier, so I decided to go slow.

As I neared the turn, I couldn't see headlights, so I moved closer to the center line. I didn't want to cross over it, but I wanted to give myself a little wiggle room, just in case. But then another silver car emerged from the fog. No lights, no warning, riding over the center line. I panicked, I swerved and punched the gas by accident. I went over the guardrail. My hands gripped the steering wheel tight as a terrified scream escaped my lips and I plummeted.

The car dropped faster than I could recall. It hit the rocks and flipped. When it did, the airbag went off. I could feel the searing heat on my arms from the abrasions, and then my head smashed against the steering wheel. A quick pinch in my neck and my eyes lost focus, going blank and dark. The last thing I could recall was water. A slow hiss of air began to escape the vehicle as I sunk lower, replaced by the darkness of the Puget Sound and ice cold, briny liquid filling the interior of my car.

***

My fingers grappled the couch. My body was weak, and twitchy. I tried my best to stand and failed. Curling into a ball, I held onto my knees and just stared into space. Gently, my body rocked back and forth without a conscious effort. Everything was dark now except for the flashes of light. They weren't nearly as bright as before, and they didn't last nearly as long now.

Through the tears, the anguish and the despair, I found a way to my feet. I looked around, everything was back to the original white design I had. The easels were gone. The pictures were missing. It looked like I didn't even live here anymore.

I called out and was greeted by silence. I made my way outside and tried calling out again. I shouted for Robbie, Kiera, Megan, Collin, Laika. Silence greeted me each and every time.

I moved towards the pier and sat in my Adirondack chair looking out at the Sound. Somewhere out there beneath the cold surface, my body lay resting in a dark, wet tomb, unrecovered.

I wasn't going to be able to see the fireworks again this next year. I wasn't going to be able to hang out here on a summer night around the fire pit with Robbie, Kiera and Megan as we discussed life. I wasn't going to be able to thank them for all their help and support. I would never be able to tell Collin how much I loved him, face to face and see his reaction. And Laika, poor Laika, would she ever understand what happened to me? I hoped she would be okay.

The last of the flashes of light were very dim, barely making a change in the tonal quality of the sky. I looked up at the clouds and realized something. Those weren't lightning flashes. They were synapses firing off and dying. I was watching my brain shut down in real time.

I laughed half-heartedly despite the sorrow.

"I get it now," I mumbled. "This was all some cosmic test, wasn't it? Every horrible thing was confronting that which I tried to cower away from in life, huh? I'm supposed to be made whole again and have some profound acceptance of life's experiences in the end? I don't get to watch my life flash before my eyes and relive the happy moments? I have to address my shortcomings and those of others I let affect me?"

There was no response. Just silence and a growing dark void.

"Yeah," My voice cracked as I tried to hold it together, one last time. "I thought so."

With a sniffle, I stood and walked to the end of the pier. The last light flashed above, and I dove into Elliott Bay, the cold no longer a concern as I disappeared into the depths. My final resting place.

ADDITIONAL ANSWERS

ABOUT THE AUTHOR:

Charley was born into a military family. From an early age he showed a keen interest in stories, storytelling and exploration. As he aged, that never changed. Through years of moving around the globe and serving in the military himself, he has had the opportunity to learn tales from various cultures, having taken experiences from far and wide to draw from, allowing him to craft his own stories. In his free time Charley enjoys photography, travelling, camping, gardening, time with his loved ones and music.

www.ingramcontent.com/pod-product-compliance
Lightning Source LLC
LaVergne TN
LVHW020711110826
845149LV00012B/2213